D1488402

AN ANCIENT FEUD . . .

"*Tonight is a glorious night!*" the black-robed acolytes sing. "*Tonight we commit the Saoshyant's body to fire!*"

My body is shackled with heavy chains. Lilith's servants march before me with their flaming torches. But my suffering will end soon. I do not struggle. I accept my fate.

"*Tonight truly is a glorious night,*" a voice whispers in my ear.

The sound is as sweet as the purest note of a flute—as familiar as my own reflection in a still pond. I know it is she. But I will not rest my eyes upon her face.

"*Don't you know why it is so special, Saoshyant?*" Lilith asks.

I will not meet her gaze!

"*Tonight is the longest night of the year. The winter solstice. A truly auspicious occasion. Tonight you begin a long sleep. And so must I. And even when you awaken, you will not remember . . . not until the anniversary of this event.*"

About the Author

Daniel Parker is the author of over twenty books for children and young adults. He lives in New York City with his wife, a dog, and a psychotic cat named Bootsie. He is a Leo. When he isn't writing, he is tirelessly traveling the world on a doomed mission to achieve rock-and-roll stardom. As of this date, his musical credits include the composition of bluegrass sound-track numbers for the film *The Grave* (starring a bloated Anthony Michael Hall) and a brief stint performing live rap music to baffled Filipino audiences in Hong Kong. Mr. Parker once worked in a cheese shop. He was fired.

COUNT DOWN

DECEMBER

by
Daniel Parker

Simon & Schuster

First Aladdin Paperbacks edition October 1999

 Produced by 17th Street Productions,
a division of Daniel Weiss Associates, Inc.
33 West 17th Street, New York, NY 10011

Cover design by Mike Rivilis

Aladdin Paperbacks
An imprint of Simon & Schuster
Children's Publishing Division
1230 Avenue of the Americas
New York, NY 10020

The text of this book was set in 10.5 point Rotis Serif.
Printed and bound in the United States of America
10 9 8 7 6 5 4 3 2

ISBN 978-1-4814-2597-1

To Jessica

DECEMBER

The Ancient Scroll of the Scribes:

In the twelfth and final lunar cycle,
In the year 5760,
Prophecies are fulfilled.
Secrets are revealed in dreams
on the winter solstice.
But the Demon stands strong.
Only the tears of humanity can defeat her,
Brushed upon the Chosen One's sword,
Which is the Demon's key to the Future Times.
Will the Chosen One prevail? Will she live
to see the Sacred Child assume her place?
Not even the Scribes know,
for that moment is blind to us.
The Chosen One can withstand all—
except the Demon's ancient weapon.
Yet the traitor may empower it,
serving the Demon in the Final Hour,
When all the earth will tremble,
When the seas will boil and
the skies will blacken.
When all of humankind will be enslaved,
Made one with Lilith—including those
who drink blood and eat flesh.
Yet the future is not set in stone.
We pray that righteousness prevails and
the forces of light smite those of darkness.

Moreover, every dead eater will bring a
violent trap as the Healer, in rhythmic
evil, is far. Twelve two ninety-nine.

The countdown has started . . .

The long sleep is over.

For three thousand years I have patiently watched and waited. The Prophecies foretold the day when the sun would reach out and touch the earth—when my slumber would end, when my ancient weapon would breathe, when my dormant glory would blaze once more upon the planet and its people.

That day has arrived.

But there can be no triumph without a battle. Every civilization tells the same story. Good requires evil; redemption requires sin. The legends are as varied as are the civilizations that spawned them—yet each contains that same nugget of truth.

So I am not alone. The Chosen One awaits me. The flare opened the inner eyes of the Visionaries, those who can join the Chosen One to prevent my reign. But in order for them to defeat me, they must first make sense of their visions.

For you see, every vision is a piece of a puzzle, a puzzle that will eventually form a picture . . . a picture that I will shatter into a billion pieces and reshape in the image of my choosing.

I am prepared. My servants knew of this day. They made the necessary preparations to confuse the Visionaries—all in anticipation of that glorious time when the countdown ends and my ancient weapon ushers in the New Era.

My servants unleashed the plague that reduced the earth's population to a scattered horde of frightened adolescents. None of these children know how or why their elders and youngers perished.

And that was only the beginning.

My servants have descended upon the chaos. They will subvert the Prophecies in order to convert the masses into unknowing slaves. They will hunt down the Visionaries, one by one, until all are dead. They will eliminate the descendants of the Scribes so that none of the Visionaries will learn of the scroll. The hidden codes shall remain hidden. Terrible calamities and natural disasters will wreak havoc upon the earth. Even the Chosen One will be helpless against me.

I *will* triumph.

PARTLY

December 2, 1999

The Twelfth Lunar Cycle

A thousand generations of waiting were drawing to a close.

Naamah had lived her entire life in anticipation of this moment—as had her mother and her mother's mother . . . a line of women stretching back into the farthest reaches of history. All of them were dead, their flesh rotted and bones turned to dust—yet the flame of their cause burned inside Naamah and every one of the Lilum who remained.

Tonight those flames would light an inferno to engulf the entire world.

Tonight Naamah and her sisters would meet their master.

The Lilum were all very young. That was the way of it. The last generation was meant to survive the insidious man-made plague—but they were also meant to bring their youth and beauty and power into the Future Time. Such was Lilith's desire.

Naamah was not even twenty. Yet in this glorious

predawn hour, hand in hand with the Lilum around the sacred fire, she felt as old as time itself. She was the final link in a chain, the living embodiment of an ancient magic understood only by the ordained. The blood that flowed in her veins was the same as that of the high priestess who first bore her name so many millennia ago, when Lilith had first walked the earth, when she whispered the dark secrets into the ears of those who would listen.

"She is Lilith," Naamah sang, "who leadeth forth the hordes from the abyss, who leadeth man to ruin!"

It was unfortunate that her mother could not live to see this moment. But the woman had understood the reasons. Before she had offered herself up in flaming sacrifice, she'd told Naamah the true nature of their sect's past and future. She'd told Naamah the story of how Lilith was the Original Woman—cast out of paradise for no other reason than that she possessed an intelligence and wanted to use it . . . cursed to three thousand years of sleep.

Yet Lilith was not content to be a slave.

Free will was the highest law. The only law.

And so before she accepted her curse, she spent a brief period wandering the globe in search of like-minded young women—those who were oppressed by ignorance and prejudice. In Greece she was known as Hecate. In Persia she was known as Angra Mainyu. In Israel she was known by her true name. Yet her message was always the same: "Join me now, and your daughters will have eternal life. They will rule the earth when I rise from my slumber."

She made enemies along the way, as all great leaders do. Those who feared her corrupted her message and inverted her words. The Hebrew prophets and Zoroastrian magi who prepared the scroll warned that she would bring darkness where there was light, death where there was life. Lies. All lies. Yet they succeeded in smuggling the scroll to a priestly family in Jerusalem, the Levy clan, who passed it down through time to the present day—as the Lilum themselves had done with their own hidden knowledge.

But Lilith took her revenge.

Was it wrong to punish those who had punished her? No. Lilith even made a copy of the scroll for herself. Yet the arcane forces who had stripped Lilith of her once exalted status made sure that one would rise to fight her again, the so-called Chosen One. . . .

A column of smoke formed in the center of the fire.

It was the sign.

The chanting voices died. The wind howled. Naamah smiled. Lilith was close. So very close . . .

"Open the circle!" Naamah cried.

Naamah let go of her sisters' hands, turning away from the fire to face the east—toward a sun that had yet to rise, toward the ancient lands where Lilith had roamed in the past.

And out of the darkness stepped a girl.

She was beautiful.

She was a teenager with long black curls, with flawless olive skin and penetrating dark eyes—with a face so stunning, so perfectly formed that Naamah felt faint with pleasure. Lilith's lips were like red wine. The curves of her body were like coiled serpents. Her dress was like a swatch of night sky.

"Lilith," Naamah whispered. She sank to her knees and bowed her head.

"Hello, Naamah."

Naamah lifted her gaze. She gasped. Tears welled in her eyes. It couldn't be. . . .

What she saw in Lilith's hands overshadowed even the awe at being in her master's presence. It was a scroll of ancient, yellowed parchment.

Not the copy. The original. The one weak link in their victory, the one potential danger that had eluded Naamah all year. First in Israel, then here in America . . . Naamah was certain that it had been lost forever.

But she should have known better. She should have known Lilith would find it. She should have known Lilith would take matters into her own hands.

"I'm sorry," Naamah wept. "I'm so sorry."

"You were supposed to find this," Lilith stated. There was a playful note in her voice, as if she were amused. "You were supposed to keep it from reaching Babylon."

"I know," Naamah whispered. She smiled through her tears. "But it doesn't matter anymore. It's safe with—"

"Oh, but it does matter," Lilith interrupted

9

gently. "The secret is out. The code was cracked. And it wouldn't have happened if you hadn't screwed up in Jerusalem. You were supposed to kill the surviving members of the Levy family." She paused. "You didn't."

Naamah shook her head, cowering under Lilith's gaze. "But we have the scroll! It can't do any harm now!"

Lilith laughed. "Probably not. I killed most of my enemies at Mount Rainier. I'll mop up the rest in Babylon." Her voice sharpened. "But it was idiotic of you to think that you would rule at my side. I rule alone. Not with an incompetent slave."

"But what about Harold Wurf?" Naamah protested in desperation. "I was the one—"

"You were the one?" Lilith cut in. "That's a big claim to make. Especially when I was the one who manipulated him, who manipulated Jezebel Howe and Caleb Walker and all the rest of them. I even manipulated the Chosen One. And you're taking credit?"

The blood drained from Naamah's face. Her eyes flashed to her sisters. But their expressions were as hard and unforgiving as the rocky earth beneath her knees.

Only then did she realize her destiny.

"Remember how your mom died?" Lilith whispered.

Naamah opened her mouth to plead for mercy. But Lilith was gone. Where she'd stood, only fire remained. Red flames danced in front of Naamah's eyes. They were upon her before she could even utter a last word on her own behalf.

CHAPTER ONE

187 Puget Drive,
Babylon, Washington
10 A.M.

Somewhere deep inside Ariel Collins's muddled and sleep-deprived brain, an idea was screaming to be heard.

Finish packing and get the hell out of the house.

The problem was that her exhausted body wouldn't listen. She couldn't keep her thoughts straight. They kept bouncing fitfully from one terrifying place to the next, like rubber balls in a diseased and rat-infested sewer. And the more belongings she stuffed into her tattered knapsack, the less progress she seemed to make. It didn't make sense. Her room was getting messier by the second. What was taking her so long?

Move it!

Okay. She took a deep breath and stood still for a moment, blinking in the painfully bright sunlight. Maybe she should close the shades. No, no. Waste of time. So what did she need? Really, truly *need?* It was a tough question. She was about to run away—and she knew she couldn't stop until she either dropped dead or got killed. So . . . a toothbrush? Sure. M&M's? Definitely. There was a bag in the kitchen. What about shampoo and deodorant and stuff like

13

that? Nah. It made no difference how she looked or smelled. There was nobody left to impress, anyway. Everyone was dead. Or gone. Or something else altogether—

The front door slammed.

Oh, no.

Footsteps pounded down the hallway.

Ariel brushed a strand of stringy brownish blond hair out of her face and rubbed her bloodshot eyes. Her breath rattled in her chest. Why had she wasted so much time? She could have left *days* ago. She could have chased after Caleb. . . .

"Ariel?"

Caleb's voice. A trick. Caleb Walker was probably halfway to Mexico by now. Her eyes darted to the window. She supposed she could jump; it was only about a twenty-foot drop.

"I know you're in here, Ariel. I saw you from the street."

She shuddered. It really sounded like him, didn't it? Of course it did. *Magic.* She was dealing with forces she couldn't even begin to comprehend. She took a step toward the window, then paused. She'd break her leg if she jumped. No . . . there was no way out. In a way, there had never been a way out. It was stupid even to *think* she had a chance.

"Look, Ariel, I knew I wouldn't be able to hide from you. I just want to know the truth, okay? You can do whatever you want—"

"Stop pretending to be Caleb!" Ariel found herself shrieking.

The voice fell silent.

She shook her head and squeezed her eyes shut. Why was the Demon torturing her like this? What was the point? It was *over*. All of it. Everything.

The footsteps moved up the stairs.

Clenching her fists, Ariel turned and marched into the hall. "If you want to kill me—"

She broke off. *Whoa.* She'd been expecting to see . . . well, she wasn't sure. But not Caleb. The illusion was perfect. Everything had been reproduced—the same broad lips and messy bangs, the same thin nose and spacey blue eyes . . . right down to the outfit Caleb had been wearing when he split: a pair of ratty jeans and a long-sleeved gray T-shirt.

He—she?—it?—paused at the top of the steps.

Ariel stared at him, every muscle tensed.

His jaw twitched. He shifted from one foot to the other, his gaze roving over her body. He looked scared—but the facial expression was probably a means of coaxing Ariel into letting her guard down. Another smart move. But Ariel wouldn't fall for it. No way. She was ready. For *anything*. Nothing could surprise her anymore. Nothing at all . . .

"Damn, Ariel," he finally whispered.

"What?"

He shook his head. "It's, ah . . . just that—well, you don't look so great."

Her mouth fell open. In spite of her fear, she laughed. "You don't look so hot yourself," she spat. "Anyway, how am I *supposed* to look? I just found out that my best friend is the goddamn Demon. So why don't you just drop the bull and show yourself?"

15

Caleb's eyes narrowed. He took a step back and glanced down the stairs. "What?"

"I know what you're doing, *Leslie*," Ariel hissed. The terror fueled her rage. "Or should I call you by your real name?"

"I . . . uh . . . ." His face grew pale.

"You're the Demon!" she shouted.

"I—I," he stammered. He stumbled on the top step, then grabbed the banister to keep from falling. "Me?"

Ariel stepped toward him. "I'd like to believe that you're Caleb," she growled. "I really would. There's only one problem. See, Caleb bolted because he thought *I* was the Demon. So it really wouldn't make much sense for him to come back, would it?"

Caleb's lips quivered.

And then he burst into tears.

"I knew you were gonna find me!" he wailed. "That's why I came back! I just want it to end, all right? Just *kill* me!"

Oh, my God. A sick feeling crept through Ariel's gut. This *was* Caleb, wasn't it? He was here to give up, to let the Demon kill him. He'd come here to end it all—just as Ariel had done only seconds ago when she'd marched out into this very hall. They were each convinced that the other was the Demon, so crazed with the horror that they wanted to die for the wrong reasons. . . .

"Kill me," he wept. "Kill me—"

"I'm sorry," Ariel blurted out. "I—I . . . I thought you were Leslie. I mean . . ."

He sniffed and glanced up at her.

"It's true." Ariel heard the tremor in her own

16

voice. "She's the Demon. She fooled us."

But the words didn't seem to register. Caleb's wet face was a blank mask.

"I can prove it," Ariel added, a little more urgently. "It's in the prophecies. It says that her name is hidden in the code, just the way those messages are—"

"Leslie?" he demanded.

She nodded. "I can show you." She grabbed Caleb's arm.

"But if Leslie's the Demon, then why . . ." He didn't finish. He pulled free of her gasp.

"Why did she go to Mount Rainier?" Ariel finished for him. Her mouth was very dry. "She wanted to kill the rest of the Visionaries. They all came to Babylon to be with Sarah—Leslie knew they'd all come here. So once Sarah was out of the way, Leslie convinced them all to go chase down that False Prophet guy. She knew the volcano was going to blow. They were her enemies. She had to get rid of them."

Caleb leaned against the wall, shaking his head. "I don't believe it," he croaked. "You're lying. I don't believe any—"

"You mean you don't *want* to believe it," Ariel interrupted. "Neither did I. But it's in the prophecies. All you have to do is look."

He didn't say anything. His entire body was trembling.

"You gotta believe me," Ariel pleaded. "She used us. Just like she used Jezebel to kill Sarah. She used us to make friends with all the kids in Babylon 'cause

17

she knew this was where everyone would end up and—"

"Stop it!" He flung out a hand. "Just . . . stop it."

Ariel drew in a quivering breath. "It's true. I know you don't want to hear this, but that's the way she planned it. She became friends with us on purpose. She became friends with *everyone* on purpose—she could make them do whatever she wanted."

He lowered his eyes.

"Her name spells Lilith," Ariel went on. "It's in the code. Leslie Arliss Irma Tisch. You take the *L*, then count four letters and take the *i*, then count another four . . ." Her voice trailed off. She could see how his face was twisting, how his lips were turning downward—and she knew the horrifying reality was sinking in.

Poor Caleb.

She had been through it all, too. That feeling of nausea, the way his skin must have been crawling at the memory of all that time spent with Leslie . . . the word *betrayal* didn't come close to describing it. There *was* no word. And in some ways Caleb must be experiencing something even worse than what she had. After all, he'd been intimate with Leslie.

"Oh, my God," Caleb murmured tonelessly.

Ariel nodded. "I know. I know."

Caleb swallowed. "You know when Jezebel stabbed you? Leslie probably set the whole thing up." He spoke as if he were talking to himself, staring down at a random spot in space, unblinking. "She made you live because she knew Jezebel would die. She wanted to have *you* as another scapegoat—so

18

people like me would think you were the Demon. People like me and that Visionary, that guy George. It worked, too."

Ariel hadn't even thought of that. But Caleb was probably right. Leslie had been there every single time Ariel should have died but didn't . . . when Ariel was stabbed, *and* when her car caught fire, *and* when she was trapped inside that burning hotel back in April. Leslie must have been keeping Ariel alive on purpose. Leslie was *toying* with her. Ariel's stomach dropped. With every hour that had passed since she had learned the truth, she ended up discovering another twisted level to the lie—

"You know, Leslie asked me to keep you away from the notebook," Caleb stated. He flashed a bitter smile. "She said all that prophecy stuff was bringing you down."

Holy—

Ariel's insides twisted again. "She didn't want anybody to crack the code," she whispered.

Neither of them said anything for a moment.

The brief relief at having convinced Caleb of the truth was quickly fading. Panic took hold of Ariel once more. They had to get out of here. She'd glanced at enough of the prophecies for this lunar cycle to know that Lilith had already won. The Chosen One was dead. Nothing stood in the way of Lilith's setting off her "weapon"—whatever the hell *that* was. And there was no point in sticking around to find out.

"What do you think we should do?" Caleb asked in the silence.

Ariel stared at him. "I think we should leave. *Now*. I was on my way out, anyway."

He nodded again. He fidgeted, glancing anxiously around the hall. "Where . . . um, where do you think we should go?"

"As far away from here as possible."

"Yeah. Take the notebook—"

"Already packed. It's with the necklace."

Caleb shot her a puzzled glance. "The *necklace?* But I thought it was gone."

"I found it on Sarah," Ariel admitted. "I didn't tell you guys because I was worried Leslie might want it back." Ariel snorted. "I was worried that it was making Leslie act strange. I was *worried* about her—can you believe it? She had me convinced the necklace had some magical power, when all along it was just *her.*"

Their gazes met. Another silence fell between them. There was nothing left to discuss. As quickly as she could, Ariel snatched her open bag off the bedroom floor—then bolted back into the hall.

Within seconds she and Caleb were on the street.

Ariel didn't bother closing the door behind her. She didn't look back.

CHAPTER TWO

**Babylon,
Washington
10:30 A.M.**

"How are you feeling?" George whispered. "You sure you don't want to get in the shade? It's not far. I can carry you."

Julia shook her head. She couldn't muster the energy to reply or even to open her eyes. The sunlight beating down on the rocky cliff had sapped all the strength from her feeble body. But she still wouldn't move. She couldn't. Rationally, she knew that the strange December heat was dehydrating her, depriving her unborn baby of vital water. Yet far more powerful was the part of her psyche that kept her from budging. *This* was the spot. Her inner pull had brought her *here*. So she remained sprawled on her back in the gravel, her head in George's lap—sweating, groaning, *praying* to give birth and get it over with. . . .

"It's okay," George soothed, stroking her matted dreadlocks. "It's okay."

I love you.

She ached to say the words. It wasn't necessary, though. He was aware of her feelings. The long months apart hadn't destroyed the invisible link

21

between them, their ability to communicate without speech. And George understood her reasons for staying in the sun. He shared them. He had also been drawn to this ocean-side bluff, pulled across the country to fulfill a vision of—

A sharp pain shot through the lower half of Julia's swollen belly.

My baby!

Her eyes snapped open. She knew this pain. It had struck her all morning . . . with greater and greater frequency, lasting longer and longer. She felt as if something were expanding inside her—then suddenly snapping shut, like a mousetrap.

What did it mean? She hadn't mentioned it. She didn't want to alarm George. It wasn't that bad. She never wanted to make people feel sorry for her, especially him. . . . Only this time her baby seemed to be *moving*. Cold sweat broke on her forehead. She struggled to sit up, blinking in the salty wind and sunshine. "What is it?" George whispered. His voice trembled slightly. She licked her dry lips. "I think I might . . ."

"Be having the baby?"

She nodded. Her heart started to pound. She couldn't catch her breath. *Lord help me.* She didn't think she'd be so scared, but now that the moment had arrived—

"Ah!" Another pain. *Contractions.* Of course. She supposed she'd known all along, but she was too frightened to accept it. Her back arched, then she slumped in George's arms. Everything faded in the shadow of the agony. But it would all be over soon.

Very soon. She was vaguely conscious of George's small face, floating against the blue sky above her—his green eyes wide with fear, his blond bangs plastered against his damp forehead.

But he wasn't looking at her. He was staring at something on the road.

"Oh, crap," he kept saying. "Oh, crap. Julia, we gotta get out of here. She's coming. We gotta get out of here."

Get out of here?

"The Demon," he whispered.

Julia squirmed in the dust, fighting to grasp what George was saying. Did he mean that he could *see* the Demon? No . . . that couldn't be right. Even through the immense torture, even though her baby was struggling to leave her womb at this very moment, Julia was lucid enough to know that the Demon was *not* that close by. The Demon was near, of course—but still many miles away. There was no immediate threat. Julia *felt* it.

"Stay away!" George yelled. He stood up and backed a few feet from Julia, toward the edge of the cliff—palms out, knees bent. "Stay away!"

"What's going on?" Julia gasped.

"I'm not the Demon," a girl answered from far away. "Just take it easy, okay?"

Julia held her breath.

The sound of that voice was . . . familiar somehow. And reassuring. Like hearing an old song. Why? Maybe Julia was delirious. Yet she was certain she knew it—as if it had drifted out of the past, like a phone call from a long-forgotten friend. The timbre stirred something hopeful inside her. The pain in her belly receded. *"I want to help."* That voice didn't belong to the Demon. Whoever had spoken was telling the truth.

"Don't come any closer," George snapped. His terrified face remained frozen before Julia's eyes. But he seemed to be fading, caught in a dreamy fog between sleep and consciousness.

A figure appeared before him. A girl. She had her back to Julia, but . . .

I know you.

A smile spread across Julia's lips. This girl was a friend.

Not in this world, but in the world of Julia's visions. In that place of darkness, in that cave she had visited so many hundreds of times, they had met. Together they'd stood by a fire. The girl had showed her a mountain. *"Remember to stay away,"* she'd warned. . . .

Mount Rainier!

Good Lord. Julia hadn't made the connection until now. That girl had been trying to keep Julia from getting killed when Mount Rainier erupted. Julia came dangerously close to the explosion—but in all the terror she'd forgotten the girl's words.

It was strange, though. Julia had always assumed that this girl was the Chosen One. But the Chosen One was dead, buried beneath a mound of stones across the road. Her name was Sarah Levy. She'd found the cure for the plague. She'd saved all their lives. . . .

"George, listen to me," the girl was saying. "I

know what you think. But I'm not the Demon. My name's Ariel. I was friends with Sarah, too." She waved at somebody beyond Julia's line of sight. "That's Caleb. We—"

"I know who you are," George spat. "Both of you."

Julia tried to open her mouth. She had to tell him about this stranger . . . this friend. She had to let him know that Ariel wasn't the Demon. But the contractions returned. She winced and squeezed her eyes shut, praying that the force of it would make her pass out. . . .

"Look into my eyes," Ariel begged. "Just look at me. You *know* I'm not the Demon, George. You're a Visionary. Can't you see it? I just want to help. This girl needs it."

Believe her, George, Julia silently commanded. *Please believe her. She's telling the truth. Deep down, you know that she is—*

"Oh, my God," George gasped. "We gotta do something! That baby's gonna die of the plague! We need something to—"

"Okay, okay," Ariel murmured fretfully. "Don't freak out. I have the cure. Some of those turnip bulbs are in my . . ."

The words were lost in Julia's own screams. Excruciating pain tore at her back. It obliterated everything else. Her organs clenched, and she cried out again, drowning out the commotion of shouting voices. Somebody was yelling to mush the bulbs; another person was telling her to *push, push*—but she was too dizzy to sort it out. Bright white bursts flashed behind her eyelids. The ground beneath her seemed to disappear, and she was left to fall through open space, down into the ocean and beyond. . . .

The fire in the cave has been extinguished. Gone, too, is the hourglass. The cave is filled with light . . . a glorious, golden light—rich and deep as a sunset. I can see the face of the girl next to me. She is no longer a stranger. I know those hazel eyes and easygoing smile. I feel as if I've known her forever.

"Ariel," I whisper.

She nods. But she looks puzzled, as if she doesn't quite understand. . . .

"I thought you were the Chosen One," I say.

She laughs. "You should have met Sarah. Then you'd know the difference."

I shake my head. "But you were the one who warned me about the mountain. Don't you remember? You told me to stay away."

She offers a sad smile. "I can't really remember anything. Not in this place. I'm not like you. I'm not a Visionary."

"But you're special. Don't you know that?"

"All I want to do is run away," she says. "How does that make me special?"

I shrug. "It doesn't matter. What matters is that we're here, and we're safe."

I want to say something else, something to make all the pain go away . . . but I can't. I know she'll fight the temptation to leave me. I know she'll stay and face the Demon.

"Can you hear that?" she whispers.

"Hear what?"

"That sound. It sounds like crying. . . ."

And I can hear it now: the shrieking wail of an infant. It grows louder and louder. The light grows brighter. Soon the cave walls are filled with a blinding glare and deafening sound, and I can't even see—

Julia sagged limply against George's shoulders. Her breath came in gasps. Her entire body was quivering, covered in sweat, *drained*. But the pain was gone. The suffering had miraculously stopped . . . as had her vision.

The screaming hadn't.

"Julia," George was whispering. She could barely hear him. "Julia. You did it. Our daughter. Our daughter . . . she's alive. You did it."

Our daughter?

She leaned back and rubbed her eyes. What was going on? How long had she been unconscious? The sun was at a different angle in the sky. Her blurred gaze wandered down to her stomach.

But there was no more bulge.

"Look at her!" George cried. He'd never sounded so elated. "She's beautiful! She's just like I saw her! Just like my visions!"

Julia glanced one way, then the other.

The landscape whirled. The distant ocean horizon spun; the tall pine trees danced with the nearby road and the gravel and shrubbery—but the baby's voice seemed to be coming from all directions at once. . . .

Two outstretched arms appeared before her.

Held delicately in them was the most amazing

creature: a human being, no bigger than a doll—with fat cheeks and a dimpled chin.

A girl.

Her toothless mouth was open wide; her eyes were closed. A small patch of slick red hair clung to her scalp. Her smooth brown skin was covered in a thin liquid film.

It was a miracle. A real, living, breathing miracle.

The fists clenched tightly at the sides of the baby's head were so *tiny*, the size of marbles. The umbilical cord still jutted from her belly—squiggly and pretzel shaped, like a little tail.

Our baby, Julia marveled. *Our daughter.* She glanced up at the girl who stood over her.

"Ariel?" she gasped. Her eyes darted back to George.

"I was wrong about her," he whispered. "Ariel pretty much delivered the baby by herself." His expression grew sheepish. "I was . . . uh, I couldn't really keep it together. I mean, it was kind of intense. . . ." He lowered his eyes.

"Here," Ariel murmured. Her brow was moist; there were dark circles under her eyes. "Take her." She leaned over and gently eased the baby into Julia's uncomprehending grasp. "Go on."

And the moment Julia took her daughter, the little girl stopped crying.

"Look at that!" George whispered.

Julia just shook her head. Holding this warm, wet body in her hands . . . it was too much. She was overwhelmed. Her emotions were like the air inside a balloon that had been stretched to the bursting point—*pop!* . . . then left to dissipate and float on the wind in an infinite number of directions. All that remained was the rent shell: empty, void, lifeless.

"She didn't need the antidote, Julia," Ariel said quietly.

"Huh?" Julia squinted up at her again.

Ariel smiled—that same melancholy smile Julia had seen in her visions. "Your baby didn't melt. The plague didn't do anything."

My God. Julia remembered what those Visionaries from Idaho had told her before they melted: *"We know about your daughter. She's the child of the Blessed Visionaries. The Chosen One will anoint her as her heir. Your daughter will lead those who defeat the Demon into a glorious New Era."*

It couldn't be true. How could the Chosen One anoint her daughter if the Chosen One was dead? And how could *this* tiny little creature defeat the Demon?

"What are you thinking?" George whispered.

Julia couldn't answer. Her thoughts were moving too fast. She stared at Ariel. "Do you feel like you know me?" she asked suddenly.

"Yeah." Ariel's smile vanished. Her face turned slightly pale. "I do."

"How?"

Ariel shook her head. "I don't know. But I'm going to find out."

187 Puget Drive,
Babylon, Washington
Afternoon

Even after several hours of begging and badgering, Ariel couldn't convince Julia to come back to her house. She couldn't even convince Julia to leave the cliff. The girl was unbelievable. Here she was—a new mother, totally exhausted, practically *dead*—yet she insisted on wilting away in the hot sun.

Yes, she was a Visionary. Yes, George had explained it: He and Julia had been drawn to this spot. Ariel understood all that. But *George* didn't seem to mind ducking inside for a little while, especially since his kid was screaming loud enough to be heard in Canada.

Finally, as luck would have it, Julia fainted.

It was a good thing, too. Caleb and George carried her back to the house and laid her down in Ariel's dad's empty bed. Ariel took charge of the baby. The unspoken thought, of course, was that the baby would cope better with a girl. Ariel didn't know if that was true or not, but the child *did* fall asleep in her arms, just like that—and slept for the entire walk home. Ariel couldn't get over how *easy* it was to hold her, to cuddle her. It was weird. She had always

31

assumed she'd be lousy with kids. She'd never held a baby in her life, much less *delivered* one.

"You're a pro," George told her as he and Caleb slumped into one of the living room couches.

Ariel shook her head. "God knows why," she mumbled.

She swayed on the balls of her feet, rocking the baby back and forth. She didn't even bother to take her backpack off. She couldn't tear her eyes from that tiny head, wrapped up in George's leather jacket, nestled against her chest.

"She's a trip, isn't she?" George asked quietly.

Ariel glanced up at him. "Don't you want to hold her?"

"In a sec." He cleared his throat. "Look . . . uh, I never got a chance to say I was sorry about freaking out earlier. First about you and then about the baby. It's just that so much stuff happened at once, and I thought . . . I mean, I thought you were . . . You know, Sarah told me—"

"It's okay," Ariel murmured. She tried to smile for his sake. He seemed so tired and frail, hunched there on the couch with his shaggy bangs in his face. Part of her wanted to cradle *him* along with his baby. Caleb, too, for that matter. She'd never seen Caleb so restless or unhappy. He couldn't even manage to look her in the eye.

"You know, um, I think I'm gonna go look for some baby supplies," Caleb mumbled. "Like formula and toys and bottles. I bet there's tons of stuff left at the mall."

George nodded. "Good idea. I'll come with you."

"Whoa, hold on a sec," Ariel protested. Her gaze flashed between the two of them as they awkwardly pushed themselves off the couch. They weren't going to leave her *alone* here, were they? What if the baby started crying again? What if Leslie suddenly decided to pay them a visit? No way. It was too risky.

"We'll be right back," Caleb insisted. But his tone wasn't so convincing. He was already halfway to the door. George was right on his heels. "We'll just go to the mall and come—"

"The mall's like an hour away!" Ariel cried. The baby stirred in her arms. She lowered her voice. "Plus it's totally looted. You won't find anything."

George and Caleb exchanged a glance.

They both hesitated.

The baby began to whine softly.

"Just wait till Julia wakes up, okay?" Ariel pleaded. "We could all use the time to rest. Then as soon as she's feeling okay, we'll *all* split, just the way we planned—"

"Hey," a groggy voice called from upstairs. "What's going on?"

Uh-oh. Ariel's shoulders sagged. Now Julia was awake. And she would probably want to go straight back to the cliff. Why couldn't these people face up to the truth? Why couldn't they get it through their heads that Lilith was still out there, that there was no stopping her, that some terrible weapon was going to go off? *Soon?*

"It's nothing, Julia," George called. "We were just going out to get some stuff for the baby. Go back to sleep."

Julia lumbered down the stairs.

"I *can't* sleep," she croaked, rubbing her puffy eyes. She yawned, then wandered over to Ariel and reached for the baby. "I think we should—"

"I think we should leave Babylon," Ariel interrupted. Her tone was soft but firm. She gingerly handed the baby to Julia. Once again, the crying abruptly and miraculously stopped. "For your daughter's sake," she added.

"We can't leave," Julia murmured, hugging the child. "Look, we're here . . . and this baby may be our only hope. There *has* to be a reason for all of this. And somehow you and I know each other. Did you figure out why?"

Ariel lowered her eyes.

"Maybe you should look at Sarah's notebook," Caleb suggested.

I know, Ariel answered silently. She *had* planned on looking at the notebook. If the answers were anywhere, they were hidden in Sarah's translation of the scroll. And she'd already figured out that Julia was one of the "Blessed Visionaries" in the prophecies. *That* was obvious.

But flipping through those pages frightened her too much.

Even if she did figure out why Julia seemed so familiar, would that help? Not really. Lilith had won. The people who had written the prophecies were aware of that possibility. They were aware that the Chosen One could die. Ariel knew the lines by heart: *"Will the Chosen One prevail? Will she live to see the Sacred Child assume her place?"* The answer was no.

34

The Chosen One was supposed to "anoint" this baby—
if the Chosen One survived. And she hadn't.

"If it's any help, I know how I know *you*," Julia
stated in the silence. "I've seen you in my visions. I
saw you in a cave. And you were confused somehow.
You didn't even know that you had helped me."

A cave? Ariel blinked. Hadn't she dreamed about
a cave once? Yeah. The memory was hazy, but she
thought she had. She remembered some other weird
stuff, too—like seeing a fire and an hourglass. And
talking to a girl. Right. A girl who asked her a question. She'd had the dream right before she saw Sarah
for the last time. . . .

"I never saw your face until today, though," Julia
went on. "And I always thought you were the Chosen
One."

"*Me?*" Ariel laughed. She couldn't help it. She
never imagined in a billion years that she'd hear *that*.
"You should have met Sarah," she mumbled. "Then
you'd know the difference."

Julia gasped. Her eyes widened.

"What is it?" George asked. He stepped toward
her. "What's wrong?"

"That's exactly what you said in my vision this
morning," Julia whispered. She stared at Ariel. "Don't
you see? We're connected in some way. There's something *special* about you."

Ariel swallowed.

Sarah had once told her the exact same thing.

"*I saw something special in you. You give off this
aura of . . . positivity.*"

It was insane. How could people like Sarah and Julia

see something special in Ariel? Everyone else figured she was the Demon, but these two—the two nicest people Ariel had ever met—*they* thought she was special.

"Julia's right, Ariel," Caleb muttered. "I mean, in one way or another, you've been at the center of this thing all along. Leslie chose *you* to be her best friend. Sarah gave *you* her notebook. That kid gave *you* that weird necklace. And you just happen to live in the place where the Chosen One and the Demon and all the Visionaries ended up. It's more than a coincidence, don't you think?"

Ariel shook her head. Maybe it *was* a coincidence. Stranger things had happened, right? Maybe this entire year was just one long freakish nightmare. *That* she could believe. Maybe she was in a coma or something. Maybe she'd hit her head on New Year's Eve while she was getting bombed with Brian and Jezebel and Jack—and her brain had misfired, creating an elaborate world where people melted and kids had visions and . . .

"Just look at the notebook, Ariel," Caleb prodded.

"Fine." She swung her backpack off her shoulders and plopped down in the beer-stained easy chair. The bag struck the floor with a heavy thud. This wouldn't take long. She'd *show* them the prophecies that said they were all about to get killed—and then, hopefully, they might reconsider leaving. She yanked out the mottled red notebook and turned to the very last page: the twelfth lunar cycle.

But the Demon stands strong,
Only the tears of humanity
can defeat her,

36

Brushed upon the Chosen
One's sword,
Which is the Demon's key to
the Future Time.

She shook her head. That old, sinking feeling was returning—that sensation of utter despair, deep in her gut. These prophecies were even more senseless and weird than any of the others. The Chosen One's sword was the Demon's key to the future time . . . which was brushed with the tears of humanity? That didn't even *mean* anything.

"What is it?" Julia murmured.

Ariel sighed grimly. "Nothing. Nothing at all."

"What about the code?" Caleb asked.

Her eyes flashed to the block of nonsense at the bottom of the page.

Moreover, every dead eater
will bring a violent trap as
the Healer, in rhythmic evil, is
far. Twelve two ninety-nine.

Wait a second. Twelve two ninety-nine. December 2. That was today. A twinge of fear shot through her. These coded passages always predicted something bad. *Really* bad. Majorly catastrophic. Like a flood, or an earthquake, or darkness, or . . .

"What's wrong?" George asked.

They were all huddling around her now, their faces creased with worry.

Her pulse picked up a beat.

"I need a . . . um, a pen," she croaked.

"Um, Ariel?" Caleb muttered. He jerked a finger at the notebook's spiral wire binding.

A ballpoint pen was jammed inside it.

The pen was right there, right in front of her face.

Ariel tried to laugh. But she couldn't. She was clearly starting to freak. *There might be nothing to worry about,* she reminded herself. The disaster wouldn't necessarily happen *here.* She had to maintain a semblance of calm—at least for George and Julia. Nobody could panic. They had a baby on their hands. She snatched the pen out of the spine and began hastily copying down the sentence underneath Sarah's translation, capitalizing the first and every fourth letter:

NoreOverEveryDeaDeatErwiLlbrAngaVio RenttRapaStheHealErinRhytHmicEvilAszaR

She paused.

What the hell? The hairs on the back of her neck stood on end. That first word looked like . . . no. It couldn't be. She scribbled only the capitals:

ΛOΣYDΣLΛVΣRSHΣRHΣΛR

"No," she whispered.

The pen slipped from her fingers and fell to the

floor. This was . . . she didn't even *know* what it was. It was wrong. She'd made a mistake. Or Sarah had made a mistake. Yeah. Sarah had made mistakes in the past. Ariel remembered reading something about it. . . .

"Ariel, what's going on?" Caleb demanded. He leaned over and squinted at the page. "What does that say? 'Moey delivers—'"

"Nothing," she interrupted.

Her heart was beating so fast now that she couldn't catch her breath. She tore back through the notebook, feverishly searching for the part about where Sarah wrote about mistranslating the text. The paper ripped as she went, but she didn't care. She had to find it. *August*. Right? It was something about—

"Who's Moey?" George asked.

"Nobody!" Ariel shrieked.

The three of them were staring at her now. She could feel their eyes, their *fear*. But even as she scoured Sarah's notes, she realized that she wasn't processing them. The words were a blur. Her moist hand smudged the ink. Her eyes glazed over. This stuff might as well have been written in Chinese.

"I think I've heard that name before," Caleb muttered.

A chill seized Ariel's body.

She couldn't even turn the pages anymore. Memories were creeping up on her, *attacking* her, but she fought them back with every ounce of strength she had. . . .

It can't be, a silent voice wailed. *It can't be*.

"It's you, isn't it?" Julia asked.

Ariel froze.

Silence fell over the room.

"I . . . ," she began. But her voice died, trailing off into nothingness.

"Oh, my God," Caleb whispered. "It *is* you. That's right. You kept calling yourself Moey when Leslie hypnotized you that time, when she got you to remember how your mother died—"

"Stop it!" Ariel gasped. Her eyes brimmed with tears. "Nobody *knew* about that name. Only my brother and my dad. And Jezebel. And they're dead. This is impossible. . . ."

"I—I don't get it," George stammered. "*You're* in the scroll?"

"No," Ariel sobbed. "It can't be right. I haven't been called Moey since I was seven years old. It was my mom's pet nickname for me. *Just* my mom's. Nobody ever used it after she died, not even my dad. Because he knew . . . because he knew . . ."

Her voice broke. She hunched over and buried her face in her hands, weeping uncontrollably. She couldn't go on.

Because he knew I killed her. He knew I murdered my own mother. He knew I didn't deserve to hear the name again because it was a term of endearment, a sign of love—

"It was an accident, Ariel," Caleb whispered. He sat on the armrest and laid a hand over her shoulder. "We *proved* it, remember? Even Trevor admitted that he was wrong. Don't you see what happened? You accidentally killed your mom, and Leslie put you in a trance and called up the memory. She twisted it to make it seem like murder. She wanted Jezebel and

40

Trevor to hate you. She wanted you to think that you *were* the Demon. And she was smart about it. She pretended to be on your side the whole time."

Ariel couldn't answer. She could only think of the name, the *name* . . . those four letters that stabbed into her chest, more painfully than the knife Jezebel had used to try to kill her. Why was that name *here*, in this book? Why had it popped up in some ancient prophecy written three thousand years ago? She wished she had never seen these pages. She wished she had never met Sarah Levy, never heard of the scroll, never cracked the code. . . . Then she would never have to face *any* of this.

"I still don't understand," George said. His voice quavered. "What does it *mean?*"

"I know what it means," Julia answered.

Ariel glanced up at her through teary eyes. "You do?"

"Yes." Julia nodded. "It means we've been wrong all along."

"About what?" she whispered.

"About the Chosen One. Sarah Levy didn't deliver my baby. You did." Julia paused. "It's *you*. You're the Chosen One."

41

PART III:

December

December 5-22

The lunar cycles were like grains of sand.

Tens of thousands of them had fallen through the hourglass. Only one remained.

The hourglass.

It was a perfect symbol, that most ancient of clocks. A perfect metaphor for the exile Lilith had endured. She had been nowhere and everywhere, asleep but awake, powerless but watchful . . . and always waiting, waiting, waiting.

Plop went a single grain, every time the moon circled the earth.

Plop . . . plop . . . plop . . .

Slow and steady. Like Lilith herself. Unstoppable. A thing of beauty. The Visionaries saw it, too. They trembled in terror before it.

Lilith breathed the night air and smiled. She marched alone on the dark pavement, ahead of her servants—maybe swaggering a little, maybe skipping now and then, even dancing when the mood struck her. But always at the same pace. She was patient. She had all night. The winding coastal highway was good for a walk. It stretched north through the woods, jutting out by the ocean, always bringing her closer and closer to where she needed to be.

I'm almost home.

The landscape was exactly how she remembered it. The only difference was the road itself. Even after three thousand years the region hadn't lost the magic—the scent of the pines, the majesty of the Pacific cliffs, that unseasonable December warmth. *Almost home.*

The circle had closed.

She had vanished here in a cloud of smoke, reappeared here in a burst of flame. And between those two moments an aeon had passed. The human race had reached adolescence. They had plundered the earth and abused one another until not a person or place remained unscathed. Progress! The modern world was a terrible, glittering machine that had finally broken down. And Lilith was here to fix it up. To purge it of its faults and bugs. To make it *perfect.* Whole. One.

It was a long time coming.

But an aeon was a blink in the eye of the universe. Superficially, a lot had changed. But human beings were no different. They never would be. The Suquamish tribespeople who had lived here three thousand years ago were just as shallow and predictable as the American suburbanites who had lived here at the end. . . .

"Who are you?" Chief Sealth asks me. "Who are you who have appeared in our midst, you who have skin as white as the clouds in heaven, eyes like black jewels?"

"I am your savior," I answer.

I smile at the warriors, the shaman, the elders who prostrate themselves before me. All are in awe.

"I have come to give you a great treasure. But you must do me a service."

Chief Sealth sinks to his knees. "Anything. Anything, Goddess!"

I wave at the cliff. "Dig a hole," I command. "Dig a hole

as deep and wide as a riverbed. I will place the treasure there. But you mustn't look upon it. You must cover it up and leave it undisturbed."

And so they dig.

They dig with their bare hands, lacking the necessary tools for the job. Hours pass. Fingers are bloodied, bones are broken, hearts fail in the heat . . . but nothing can deter them from completing the task I have ordered. They are the perfect servants.

They set the trap, not knowing that their crime will be forgotten. Their tribe will be wiped from existence in the distant future. All tribes will be destroyed as the United States spreads west, swallowing everything in its path. Only the weapon will remain. . . .

Lilith grinned. The poor Suquamish. They served her so well. They were such a superstitious breed.

Just like the Visionaries.

She'd never made the comparison before—but then, a comparison like that could be made with anyone. As she'd said: People were people. And the Visionaries were *kids*, no less. The energy of the solar flare might have blessed them with ESP, but they were still human. Why else would they have gone to Mount Rainier without any protest? Nobody even asked *why*. She'd planted the ridiculous idea in their minds that stopping the False Prophet would somehow serve the Chosen One. And off they'd run.

It also helped that Leslie Arliss Irma Tisch was such a fine-looking young woman.

The Visionaries were like dogs with their tongues hanging out of their mouths, quick with a smile and a *yes, yes, yes.* Anything to please Leslie. People loved making pretty girls happy. Even other girls. It was a simple fact of human nature, and one that had served Lilith quite well.

Almost home.

After a few more steps she paused. She could hear the weapon humming, beckoning to her, whispering on the night breeze like an old boyfriend: *Just a little bit longer, babe. Just a little bit longer.*

She turned around and waved. "Come here," she called.

One by one, dozens of torch-bearing girls appeared out of the darkness. They formed a circle around her. Like Lilith herself, they were all beautiful. True, they were flawed and spoiled and egotistical—but they looked good. They smiled at her.

Even in their black robes, they were hot. *Smoking.* Yeah, baby!

Lilith loved the vernacular of the modern age, the slang. It was so expressive. On point. Not stilted like the languages of the past. She could listen to the Chosen One talk for hours. What *would* the Chosen One say about these chicks? *"Uh, Leslie, I hate to break it to you, but those robes are totally wack. I hate them. Goth is, like, so five years ago."*

She and the Chosen One were really two of a kind. Both loved a good time. Both were murderers. Both were immortal.

Well, *almost* immortal, anyway. They each had one little weakness—

"Dark moon, Lilith!" her servants chanted in unison.

Lilith nodded tiredly. Her servants never lightened up.

They insisted on formality. Like those rituals they performed—did they really think that she *cared?* Did they honestly think she gave a crap about a circle of stones painted with lame pictures of owls and crescent moons? And all the rhyming blather in Hebrew and Aramaic and a dozen other dead tongues . . . it was so silly, really. None of it had any effect on *her.*

On the other hand . . . ritual did have its place. Superstition kept the Lilum in line. Just as it had the Suquamish. And the Visionaries. It filled them with a sense of power. Yes, the power was false, but human beings loved trying on different identities and living hidden lives.

They loved lying to themselves.

At the very least Lilith had done a good job when she'd picked her servants' lineage. There would be no room for ugliness in the new era, no room for blemishes upon the face of perfection. These girls represented beauty from every corner of the globe. They were all united by their attractiveness. *And* they were united by the secrets Lilith had shared with their ancestors, the secrets that laid the foundation for the coming victory.

She still kept the best secret to herself, of course. Not even the weak-minded fools who'd inscribed the magic scroll with their hidden codes and prophecies knew the *true* nature of the world to come. But a surprise was always much more fun, wasn't it?

Hell, yes!—as the Chosen One would say.

"I have some business to take care of," Lilith announced.

"What kind of business?"

Amanda. Lilith smiled. It was a bold question—especially coming from a servant who had failed her in the past. The failure hadn't been a minor one, either. If Amanda had fulfilled her duty, the Sacred Child would never have been conceived. George Porter and Julia Morrison would have died in February. Lilith would have nothing to fear.

Not that she was afraid. Annoyed was more like it. Annoyed that all of the prophecies had come true so far when *she* could have controlled her own fate. . . .

"I'm sorry," Amanda murmured. "It's not my concern."

"Of course it is," Lilith answered gently. "All for one and one for all, right?"

A few of the Lilum laughed. But Amanda kept silent. Lilith peered into her mind. Good. Amanda was remembering Naamah—how Naamah had also disappointed Lilith and how she had paid for the disappointment with her life. Little did Amanda know that she would pay, too . . . but in a much subtler way. All of the Lilum would meet the same destiny. For some it would be a reward. For others, like Amanda, it would be a punishment. In the end it didn't matter. Reward and punishment would be the same: just words, meaningless distinctions from a forgotten time—like the gibberish of the Prophecy Codes.

"We have one little problem," Lilith continued. "An inconvenience."

"The key to the Future Time?" Amanda asked fearfully.

Lilith nodded. "I let Sarah Levy take it before she killed Jezebel Howe. I didn't want to arouse the Chosen One's suspicions. I thought I'd be able to get it back. I didn't expect her to crack the code—the scroll had been taken away from her. But thanks to Naamah, the Chosen One received Sarah's translation of the scroll. She figured out who I really am. She told the Blessed Visionaries."

None of the Lilum uttered a word. In the torchlight Lilith could see worry on every one of their faces. She suppressed a sneer. The reaction was so ... *human*.

"There's nothing to worry about," Lilith said with an impatient sigh. "She won't figure out how George and Julia's baby poses a threat to me. But she won't exactly hand over the necklace if I ask for it. So we're going to have to follow the prophecies."

"You mean the traitor?" Amanda asked.

Lilith nodded again. "The traitor."

And again there was silence.

Lilith read her slaves' collective thoughts. They were very concerned now. They knew that she had to *talk* to the traitor—which might mean risking contact with the Sacred Child.

But Lilith understood the risks better than any of them. What did they think she'd been doing for the past eight months? She hadn't been sitting on her ass, that was for damn sure. She'd been putting the pieces in place. Setting them up for a checkmate. She *knew* the traitor. In the biblical sense, no less. She'd seduced him on numerous occasions.

He was nothing more than a puppet.

Did they really think she would jeopardize her own existence? Did they really think she would expose herself to the one thing that could possibly destroy her?

She snorted. The whole situation was ridiculous, really. Laughable. Even the Chosen One would agree. All the armies of the world couldn't kill Lilith . . . but the tears of a newborn baby could.

So she had to keep her distance.

But such was the nature of the curse.

Bah. There was no point lamenting her predicament; it couldn't be changed. Still, the ancient magic was so needlessly cruel in some ways. Not only for Lilith—but for the Chosen One as well. And for all of humanity. The big difference was that humanity had brought *its* curse upon itself. Lilith had committed no crime. Yet still she had to suffer. . . .

"What's your plan?" Amanda asked.

"Don't worry," Lilith replied. "It's all under control."

She chuckled. As if she would actually tell *Amanda* what she had in mind.

CHAPTER FOUR

Babylon,
Washington
December 4–6

December 4

So. How do I even start?

I spent all night going through my journal, reading all the stuff I wrote over the past year, and those are the very first words I put down. "So. How do I even start?" Page 1: January 1. I guess that means I've come full circle. Nothing's changed, at least as far as my feelings go. I'm just as burnt-out and confused and scared as I was back then, back when I had no idea what was going on, when I was just like everyone else.

I still can't bring myself to say it.

I thought I could write it down, but I can't even do that. I keep hoping something will prove Julia's theory wrong. I've gone through Sarah's journal, too. Again and again and again. I must have looked at the prophecies a hundred times, trying to find just *one* little part that doesn't fit, *one* little thing that doesn't match.

But I can't. And I started figuring some stuff out. Stuff I didn't want to know. Like I'm pretty sure that the necklace *does* have powers. The prophecies say that Leslie stole the "key to the future time" from me in September, which was when she borrowed the necklace.

They must be the same thing.

But why did she give the necklace to Sarah? There's nothing in the prophecies about it. It's one more mystery, I guess. I'm just glad I got it back.

Anyway, I also figured out why all those Visionaries kept vaporizing whenever they got near me. They denied that I was the Chosen One. The prophecies in may say that the people who deny me to my face "will surely perish."

I guess I'm admitting it, aren't I? I'm saying "me." But I didn't want those kids to die. It wasn't their fault they didn't believe in me. I didn't believe in me, either. I spent all that time making fun of the "COFs," the "Chosen One freaks." Me and Leslie. We were a regular dis factory, churning out the put-downs. I want to blame her, but I can't. I was just as guilty.

I better not think about it. I've got to concentrate on answering more questions. Like what happened to Jezebel? Did she just flip out? Did Leslie make her go crazy? Or is she the "traitor" the prophecies keep talking about? And if she is, then why is she dead?

December 5

Julia and I had a really cool talk this morning. She even made me feel better about being, you know . . . whatever

Well, maybe not <u>better</u>. But I'm coming to terms with it.

I relate to her in the same way that I related to Sarah. We just have this bond. I can't describe it, but it's there. Julia said that normal people sometimes find themselves in incredible circumstances, and they just have to step up and accept it. They don't have a choice. That's how she looks at being a Visionary. That's how she looks at being a mother.

She told me that I should look at being the Chosen One in the same way.

She said this whole year, she kept feeling like she was starting over. She thought that the world was one way, and then it would turn out to be something totally different. So she got used to it.

It was like she was reading my mind.

seriously. I felt like she was expressing everything that I've kept inside me this whole time. I'm not doing any justice to how she said it because it was really beautiful and poetic. Not cheesy at all.

But I never really did have a way with words, did I?

December 6

I can't get over how beautiful the baby is. They still haven't named her. She has the most incredible eyes. One is green, and the other is brown. She looks so much like Julia.

People used to say that I looked a lot like my mother.

Julia told me that I have to make peace with Mom's death. She says that was why the name "Noey" was encoded in the scroll. It was a way of letting me know that I wasn't responsible for

killing Mom and that I have to take
my hurt and loss and turn it around.
In a way, I have to assume my mother's
role. For everybody. I'm the Chosen One.
I'm the head of the family. And the
family is what's left of the human race.

That's what the last coded message
really means. According to Julia,
anyway. Pretty deep, huh? I don't know
if I believe her, but she got me to stop
crying.

December 7

We've settled into a weird little
routine, the five of us. George and
Julia and the baby hang out in the
living room. Caleb lies around in
Trevor's bed, staring up at the ceiling
and saying nothing. And I sit here
holed up in my bedroom, studying the
prophecies.

I guess I've made a little more

progress. I know why I survived Jezebel's knife attack.

Apparently nothing can kill me except the Demon's weapon. Not that I feel good about it. I don't know what the Demon's weapon is, so I guess I'm in big trouble. Or maybe I'm not. Maybe I'll live forever. But somehow that doesn't exactly sound so appealing.

It's weird. People always used to say What would you do if you could live forever? Well, not always. Actually, I think Jezebel only asked me that once when she was wasted. I didn't have an answer then, and I don't have one now, either. I only know that the possibility of being around forever scares the crap out of me. I think I would be really bored and lonely.

I also figured out why Sarah thought that <u>she</u> was the Chosen One. I can't blame her at all. She went through a lot of the same stuff that I did. So a bunch of the prophecies fit her, too. The coincidences are pretty incredible. She was separated from her brother at the same time I was. Jezebel stole the scroll from her when Leslie took the necklace from me. . . .

She also mistook the dates in the code as dates marking stuff that happened to her personally. That's what really clinched it for her. Like when she met Abrahim. She thought "two twenty ninety-nine" was in the scroll because that was the day Abrahim saved her life. It was natural for her to think that. But she didn't know the code. That date was only in the scroll because of "rain in the Sahara."

It's so unfair. But in a way, I'm glad she died thinking she was the Chosen One. She deserves to feel good about herself. She deserves the best.

No, actually, screw that.

What she _really_ deserves is to be alive, and happy, and studying journalism in Israel like she wanted. And Leslie took all that away from her.

Caleb just left to look for baby supplies. George and Julia said it might be dangerous for him to go out on his own, but he said he'd be careful. I didn't argue. I think they're wondering why I let him go. I can't tell them why, though. I don't even want to admit it to myself.

I think Caleb might be the "traitor."

I've been thinking a lot about this. It's the only way the prophecies really make sense. Like in May, the scroll said the traitor was in my midst when I "led my companions to death and ruin." That was when Trevor shot everyone at the college. Caleb was one of the few who got away. Then in July, Caleb and I got in that huge fight, and the prophecies said that the traitor would bring "woe" to me. And he did. He dissed me hard. August, too. August was when he ditched me for good and I split town and Leslie used me and

Okay. I'm getting hysterical. But the prophecies hold together. All of them.

Or do they? Am I just imagining things?

I'm scared. Caleb seems distant and depressed, just the way he did in July. He's hiding something. I know it. Maybe that's why he came back to find me in the first place. Maybe he knew I was the Chosen One all along. Maybe he and Leslie have been in on this from the start.

I'm not going to tell George and Julia. I don't want to freak them out

any more than I have to. I'm just
going to play it cool.

Anyway, I have a feeling Caleb will
be just fine out there, looking for baby
supplies. I don't think he has anything
to worry about.

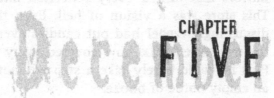

CHAPTER FIVE

**Old Pine Mall,
Babylon, Washington
Afternoon of December 8**

As a guy who had been a major troublemaker pretty much all his life, Caleb Walker was familiar with returning to the scene of a crime. He knew how it felt. He didn't go through any guilt, exactly. No, he hadn't experienced *that* emotion until fairly recently. It was more like . . . excitement. And fear. And the dread of being discovered, if he hadn't been caught already. And since he rarely *did* get caught—then, of course, it was the awesome satisfaction of knowing that he'd done something bad and gotten away with it.

But standing here in this toy store . . .

For starters, he couldn't really call it "the scene of a crime." That would be sugar coating it just a little. The things he'd done in here were to "crime" what "mass murder" was to "parking violation." So satisfaction didn't really play a part in this case.

But it wasn't just the twisted, depraved, *sickening* wrongs he'd committed—without even knowing how bad they really were. It was the place itself. It was the whole evil *atmosphere* of the joint: the shelves full of leering masks, the action figures with their miniature axes and assault rifles, the dust-covered fun house mirrors that turned every reflection into a bad trip. This store was a vision of hell. Even the floor was disgusting. Jezebel had put candles everywhere, and the misshapen wax now covered every square inch. Plus he could barely take a step without tripping on an empty bottle of booze.

Crunch went the glass as he tiptoed forward.

At least it was dark. That helped. Not much, but a little. *Pop! Ping!* Hardly any sunlight penetrated this deep into the mall. It might as well have been midnight. But it always *felt* like midnight in the toy store, didn't it?

Why did I come back?

Toys. Right. *That* was it. He couldn't get distracted. He was on a mission. He wasn't here to reminisce. The past was over. He was here for the future. There were enough toys in this place to keep Julia and George's daughter occupied every single day of her life—if she ever got the chance to grow up. Toys for toddlers. Toys for kids ages three to nine. Toys for kids ages twelve and older. One for everybody. He would fill his arms with toys and go back to Ariel's house, then do it again and again . . . until every last item was cleared out.

Going out of business! Everything must go!

And by getting the toys *here*, he was making a symbolic gesture. He was taking something that represented evil and turning it into something positive. It was the first step toward getting his life back on track. Next would come the confessions. Yes, sir. He would tell Ariel everything: that he had fooled around with Jezebel behind her back, that he was a liar. It would hurt, but he would do it. The truth would set him free. Then he would make the hardest confession of all—

Whoosh!

Caleb froze.

He stopped breathing.

Fiery orange light filled the room. He squinted at the sudden brightness. *What*—

The candles in the store were suddenly aflame. *All* of them. Dozens. *My God.* His pulse tripled. All the little wax stumps had leaped alive at the exact same moment. . . .

"Hey, Caleb."

His legs gave out instantly, as if they were jelly.

He collapsed to the floor. Broken glass sliced his fingers, but he hardly noticed. Panic numbed the pain. He tried scrambling back, but it was no use. His head slammed into one of the shelves, knocking a bunch of stuffed animals from their perch. They tumbled down on top of him. He was trapped. *Trapped.* Leslie was standing right there. Right in the aisle. Not five feet away. Smiling. Wearing that slinky black miniskirt. *Oh, God, no. Oh, God . . .*

"Neat trick, huh?" she asked.

He gaped up at her, motionless.

"Oh, come on," Leslie murmured. "Don't be scared."

His chest burned. For a second he thought he might be having a heart attack.

"What . . . what do you want?" he choked out.

"Just to talk," she said. She sounded almost apologetic. She kicked a few shards of glass out of her way, then sat cross-legged on the floor, facing him. "I'm sorry, Caleb. I didn't mean to freak you out. Really. I just wanted to create a little ambiance. Now that the secret is out, there's no point hiding what I can do, right? I thought lighting the candles would be a nice touch."

The pain beneath his ribs intensified. The sound of his own pounding heart filled his ears. He should have listened to George and Julia. He should have stayed home. But he wanted so badly to make up for everything—

"Easy," she soothed. "It's okay. Remember what I said the last time we were in here together? It's over between us. Sure, we have something special, but—"

"We don't have *anything!*" he shouted.

Her lips curled in a little grin. "Okay. But I just wanted to explain some stuff to you. You've got a right to know what's going on. What's *really* going on."

Caleb blinked a few times. Gradually his heart rate began to slow down. He couldn't believe it. She was really amazing. She didn't look or sound any different. No horns, no fangs—just the same old Leslie. Here she was, some all-powerful Demon who had destroyed the entire world . . . and she still could make him feel relaxed, as if he were simply talking to an old girlfriend.

"So?" he whispered. "Tell me."

"Well, for one thing, if you know about *me*, I guess you know about Ariel, too. She's this so-called Chosen One." Leslie rolled her eyes, forming little quotation marks in the air with her fingers. "Believe me, that's not *my* name for her. It's just what the people who wrote that stupid scroll called her."

68

Caleb swallowed. "What *is* your name for her?"

"Um . . . Ariel Collins?" She smirked. "I think that's what you call her, too."

His eyes narrowed. Was that supposed to be funny?

"Look," she continued, "I'm just trying to tell you that you have the wrong idea. About *both* of us. I'm not some wicked monster, and Ariel isn't some pure-as-snow savior. The problem is that the people who wrote those prophecies saw the world in black and white. They were pretty simpleminded, you know? Dumb, even. The truth is that Ariel and I aren't that different." She chuckled. "Come on, Caleb. You *know* us."

"I *thought* I knew you," he countered shakily.

She sighed. "I hate to say it, babe, but you *do* know me. What you see is what you get. I may be able to snap my fingers to light a bunch of candles, but I'm not much of an actress. I haven't been around people long enough to pretend I'm something that I'm not."

"What are you *talking* about?" he shouted, forgetting his fear. He couldn't believe this. She obviously thought he was an idiot. "You've been pretending to be something else from the day I met you. You pretended to be some girl named Leslie. A girl. Not a demon."

She shook her head. "That girl named Leslie is me, Caleb," she murmured. "The word *demon* is a label that somebody else made up. That's all it is: a word. I don't like it any more than you do. The only difference between you and me is that I'm going to be around forever. And that doesn't even have to be a difference."

For several long seconds he simply stared at her. *Doesn't have to be a difference?* What was she talking about? He couldn't understand her. It was as if she were mumbling through a distorted amplifier and only a fraction of her words was getting through. Maybe he *was* an idiot. Was she offering him something?

Leslie smiled again. "Here's the deal, all right? On December 31, some major stuff is gonna go down. And it *isn't* gonna be some big battle between Ariel and me. It doesn't have to be, anyway. We can all be together. We can all be happy. But if I'm gonna have any control over what happens, I'll need the necklace."

He blinked. His lips pressed into a tight line. This wasn't good. Ariel had said that Leslie might want the necklace back. But Ariel didn't know *why*—

"The thing is, I know she won't give it to me," Leslie added casually. Her voice was very calm—as if she were talking about something as trivial as borrowing a shirt. "She'll probably think I'm lying. So you have to snag it for me."

His face twisted into a scowl. "I have to snag it for you," he echoed flatly.

"Right."

"So let me get this straight," he hissed. "*You* want *me* to steal the necklace from Ariel. Do I have the word *chump* written on my forehead? Do I?"

Her face fell. She actually looked hurt. The *gall* of this chick, of this demon, or whatever she was . . . it was unbelievable.

"You're not understanding me, Caleb," she said.

"I guess not," he barked.

"All I'm saying is that if I have the necklace, I'll be able to use its power." She spoke very quickly. "We'll *all* survive this thing. You, me, Ariel . . . and everyone else who's left. We won't just survive, either. We'll turn this world into paradise. No more fear, no more death. If *I* have the necklace, I can make us live. Forever. I can turn the words of the prophecies around so they work for all of us."

Caleb shook his head. "Pretty easy. All I have to do is give you what you want . . . and we'll all live forever. Ariel, too. In paradise."

Leslie shrugged.

"But what you're really saying is that I have to betray Ariel," he stated. His voice hardened. "You're saying that I have to trust *you*. After all the lies and tricks. You made me think that Ariel was the Demon. Then you made me think that Jezebel was the Demon. So tell me, *Lilith* . . . why the hell should I believe you now?"

"Oooh," she teased. Her tone had abruptly changed. It was mocking, sarcastic. She leaned away from him and held up her hands, pretending to be scared. "Betrayal. That's a big word. Look, Caleb, I don't deny lying to you. I did what I had to do. If you knew that I was the Demon from the start, I wouldn't have been able to pull this off. Right?"

Caleb glared at her. He kept his mouth shut. He wasn't going to play her game.

She grinned. "But as far as making you believe in something . . . I had nothing to do with that. *You*

71

were the one who thought Ariel was the Demon. Then Sarah convinced you that the Demon was Jezebel. *I* always argued on Ariel's behalf, remember? *I* was the one who chased you down and made you come back to her, remember?" A very unpleasant sensation gripped his stomach.

Leslie's accusations weren't fair. Of *course* he'd believed that Ariel was the Demon. That was why he'd run away. . . .

"And while we're on the subject, why the sudden change of heart about *betraying* Ariel? Or about lying, for that matter. You cheated on her in this very store. Not just with me, but with Jezebel, too—"

"Shut up!" he snarled. "You . . . you—you're twisting everything around!"

She laughed, but her brow was knit. "Am I? Just last month you made a move on me. I had to convince you that you and Ariel were meant for each other. I *still* believe that. I mean, think about all the stuff you have in common. You both love to party. You both love M&M's. And neither of you are ever really completely honest with yourselves—"

"Shut up," he repeated. But the words had lost their edge. He closed his eyes and rubbed his temples. Why couldn't she just leave him alone? He couldn't listen to this crap; he couldn't think straight anymore. He felt as if his brain were overheating with anger and frustration and terror.

She touched his knee. "I'm sorry. I'm not trying to be mean. I'm only trying to tell you that people are all the same. Myself included. And you know it. Nobody's better than anyone else. Remember what

72

you told me? You said, 'You're not a bad person. There's no such thing. *Everybody's* a little bad. Everybody's a little good, too.'"

Ugh. He wasn't just queasy anymore—he was on the verge of puking. He *had* said that stuff, hadn't he? And he still believed it. But he wouldn't admit that. Not to her. She was trying to manipulate him. He wouldn't even open his eyes. . . .

"You're a smart guy, Caleb," she whispered. "That's part of the reason you've made it this far. And you know that I'm right. So all you have to do is bring me the necklace on December 31. I'll be waiting for you on that cliff where George and Julia had their baby. Bring Ariel, too. Just don't tell her what you plan to do—'cause we both know she'll flip out. Okay?"

Go away. Go away. Go away—

"Oh, one more thing. I left you a van outside in case you want to bring some of these toys to the baby. Just as a little token of goodwill. You can load it up. I figure it would be easier than making a bunch of trips back and forth to Ariel's house." She patted his knee one more time. "See you on New Year's Eve. Get ready for some fun."

Bile rose in his throat. This was too much. He opened his eyes. "Why are you—"

But nobody was there.

He was all alone in the toy store.

The candles had been extinguished, as if nothing had ever happened.

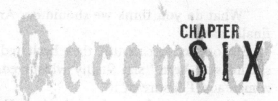

CHAPTER SIX

187 Puget Drive
Babylon, Washington
Early morning of December 9

"I really think we should go looking for him," Julia mumbled, peering through a crack in the curtains out into the dark street. "The sun will be up soon. Maybe we should—"

"It's too dangerous, Julia," George interrupted quietly. "Anyway, I don't think we'll find him. I don't think he's coming back."

Ariel bit her lip. She glanced between the two of them in the dim candlelight. Their voices carried an odd stiffness. They were avoiding eye contact. She'd never seen them act like this—so tense and clumsy around each other. George's back was rigid in the easy chair. His jaw was tightly set, his eyes down on his lap. And Julia kept pacing around the room, clutching their sleeping baby like a life preserver.

It's me, Ariel thought grimly. She fidgeted in the couch, drumming her fingers on her knees. *I'm making them nervous. They're wondering why I'm so quiet. They're waiting for me to say something about Caleb, to take charge of the situation—anything. Maybe I should just tell them the truth. . . .*

75

"What do you think we should do, Ariel?" George finally asked.

She opened her mouth, then hesitated. "I think we should stay here," she finally whispered. "Caleb will come back. I'm sure of it."

Julia turned from the window. "Is something bothering you, Ariel? I mean, besides the fact that Caleb is missing?"

Uh-oh. Ariel shook her head. "Not, uh—not really," she stammered. Great. *That* was convincing. But what was the point of lying, anyway? She couldn't hide anything from these two. They were Visionaries. Powerful Visionaries. *Blessed* Visionaries. They could probably read her mind. They could definitely read each other's minds. She wouldn't be surprised if they only said stuff out loud for *her* benefit, so she wouldn't feel left out.

"It's Caleb, isn't it?" George asked pointedly. His hard green eyes bored into her own. "There's something about him you don't trust."

"I just . . ." She sighed. "I just don't really want to talk about it, I guess."

"But you *have* to," Julia murmured. She sat down on the couch beside Ariel, bundling the baby up in her arms. "You can't keep secrets from us. It's too late for that. We all have to help each other out."

Ariel lowered her eyes, staring at one of the candles. She couldn't bring herself to say it out loud. It was the same problem she had with accepting that *she* was the Chosen One. Because if she said that Caleb might be the traitor, that would make it real—even if by some miracle it wasn't true. Once the idea was out in the open, it could never be forgotten or ignored. Ever. The suspicions would always linger. . . .

"Well, *I* don't trust him," George muttered. "There's something going on there. I saw it the day I met him. He was all smiles for Sarah, kissing her butt—but it was bull. He was scared of her. He does what he has to do to get by. No matter what." He laughed harshly. "Believe me, I know the type."

But Caleb's not like that, Ariel protested in silence. She kept her eyes fixed on the dancing flame. *He never kisses anyone's butt. He's always been honest with me. He wanted to run away with me. And now that he knows that I'm the Chosen One . . .* But she knew she was trying to deny what she feared most. And with every passing second that Caleb remained out *there,* that fear seemed more and more justified.

Who better to betray the Chosen One than the person the Chosen One loved most?

"Can I ask you guys something?" she whispered. "What do you think it *means* to be the Chosen One? Because I've gotta be honest with you. I have no idea."

Julia and George glanced at each other. They looked scared.

"What it means?" George asked cautiously.

"Yeah." Ariel sat up straight, relieved to change the subject. "Like, why am *I* involved in any of this? Why do you need me? And I don't mean just you guys—I mean . . . everyone. Why am I needed at all? Because it seems like you're the ones who should be able to beat the Demon. You've got the visions. You've got the baby. You're the ones . . ." The sentence hung in the air, unfinished. She shook her head. She didn't even know what she was trying to say.

George's eyes narrowed. "You aren't thinking about splitting again, are you?"

"No." Ariel slumped back in the couch. "I'm sorry. That came out wrong. It's just I still don't know how I fit in." Her eyes flashed to Julia. "Like, you say that you saw me in your visions, and I *still* didn't know what was going on. Why not?"

Julia tried to smile, but her expression seemed pained. "I don't know. But I knew you. I recognized you. And you helped me. That's the important thing. Anyway, that was only one of my visions. I've had others, too."

"Like what?" Ariel pressed.

"Like . . . I saw myself in a desert, stabbing the Demon with a sword," Julia said. She stared off into space, absently stoking her baby's thin tufts of red hair. "She didn't look like a girl, either. She looked like a real demon, covered in fire, with these awful black eyes and—"

"But that's exactly what I'm talking about," Ariel interrupted. She shrugged hopelessly. "You saw *yourself* killing the Demon. Not me. *You.* So where do I come in?"

Julia's eyes wandered over to Ariel, then drifted away again. "That's what we have to figure out. It must have something to do with the prophecies. You showed us, remember? It says that *you're* the one who kills the Demon with a sword . . . or the key to the Future Time."

Both, Ariel thought dismally. *It says the sword is the key to the Future Time. But the key to the Future*

Time is the necklace. It makes no sense. Is a necklace a sword? Not the last time I checked.

"Don't let this get you down, Ariel," Julia said. "I *know* you'll figure it out. You're always the one who figures things out, who handles the tough situations. That's where you come in. Think about all the stuff you've done. You cracked the code. You delivered my baby. You're a *leader*. I can see it, and I know George can, too."

Ariel's shoulders sagged. A leader. Sure. If she was a leader, then why did she feel like crawling into a hole and dying? Maybe Julia's words had been true—*once*, a long time ago, in a different world . . . where being a leader just meant being hip and aloof enough to intimidate people. But that wasn't even *leadership*. It was ego. Ariel just liked being the center of attention. She always had. That was why she'd hated Leslie so much when they'd first met. Well, that and the way Caleb had drooled all over her. But Leslie posed a threat to Ariel's social status: with her looks, with her humor, with *everything*. And then Ariel had come under her spell, too. . . .

"We still haven't answered the Caleb question," George stated. His tone was flat. "You gotta tell us what's on your mind. I mean, if you know something about that dude that's—"

He broke off suddenly and turned toward the window. "Hey. You hear that?"

Jeez. Ariel held her breath, instantly forgetting the conversation. Was that a *car* on her street? It sounded like one: the roar of a motor, growing louder and louder. . . . Yup. No doubt. She could see the headlights now, too—lighting up her drawn curtains, sweeping across the room.

Tires screeched. The engine died. A door slammed.

"Who is it?" Julia hissed. She shot Ariel a frightened glance.

Ariel shook her head, eyes wide. "I don't know—"

The front door crashed open.

"Caleb?" Ariel cried. *Oh, my*—

He looked terrible. He staggered into the room without closing the door, panting—his stringy brown hair damp and tangled, his ratty clothes reeking of sweat. His skin looked like ash. He was literally *gray*. His wild eyes flashed among the three of them.

"What took you so long?" George demanded. "Where did you get the wheels?"

"Leslie," he gasped. He shook his head. "Leslie . . ."

Ariel's blood turned to ice. "Leslie?" she asked. "What about her?"

Caleb shook his head in quick, jerky motions. "She gave me this van. She . . . she . . ."

"What?" George barked. "Spit it out!"

"She found me at the mall," he whispered. He ran a hand through his hair and swallowed. "She told me all this crazy stuff." His gaze zeroed in on Ariel. "She wants the necklace back. She wants me to steal it from you and bring it to her on New Year's Eve. On that cliff. She told me to get it . . . and then she just disappeared."

Ariel blinked. He was speaking almost too fast for her to follow. Was this a confession? She had no idea whether he was telling the truth or not. He'd definitely had *some* kind of encounter with Leslie. She was sure of it. That kind of fear couldn't be faked. So was he scared enough to betray Ariel? Or had he already betrayed her? Had Leslie threatened him in some way? And why had she given him a *van?* It was crazy—

"Why does she want the necklace?" George demanded.

Caleb kept his gaze fixed on Ariel. "She said she needs to use it to turn the prophecies around to work for all of us. She says we can all be happy. Together."

"She's lying," Ariel whispered. "She needs the necklace for something bad. . . ."

"I know. I know." Caleb shook his head again. He was shivering. "Look, I, uh . . . I have some toys for the baby," he mumbled. "And one of those fold-up cribs—"

"Shut up," George growled. He jabbed a finger at Caleb's chest. "Don't try to weasel your way out of this. Answer the goddamn question. *What* did the Demon say to you?"

"I told you." Caleb took a deep breath. "She told me all these lies. Then she was like, 'If you want to take these toys, there's a van outside.' She was totally cool and nice and laid-back, just like always. Then she just disappeared."

Ariel stared at him.

He stared back. Nobody said a word.

Man. She let out a deep breath.

He *was* telling the truth. He was too scattered, too shaken to make this up. Besides, she could usually tell when somebody was hiding something—as he'd been before today. There was always a little hint, a subtle giveaway: restless eyes, strained voice. . . . But in spite of Caleb's obviously

81

distracted behavior, he wasn't lying now. No.

She felt a flicker of hope. This was real. And that meant Leslie had *tried* to turn him into a traitor—but he'd refused. So that answered the question in the prophecies. Right? The "blind moment" was visible now. The traitor *wouldn't* serve the Demon. Caleb knew that Leslie was trying to trick him. He'd made up his mind to tell Ariel. . . .

"I've had enough of this crap," George suddenly snapped. He lunged across the room and shoved Caleb against the stairwell banister. "If you—"

"Stop it!" Ariel shrieked.

Both boys froze—fists raised and eyes slitted, breathing between clenched teeth.

The baby started to whimper.

Jeez. Ariel jumped up and stormed across the room. "What's your problem?" Her gaze darted between the two of them. "Look at you! This is so stupid! You're acting like . . . like *animals.*"

"But he's a liar!" George protested. "And I want to know what he's been up to."

The baby's cries grew more plaintive.

"He hasn't been up to anything," Ariel barked.

George lowered his arm. "How do you know?"

"I know because I know *him,*" Ariel answered, her voice softening. She looked into Caleb's eyes—those wonderful, sparkling, boyish blue eyes . . . and saw the understanding there. No words needed to be exchanged. He *had* made his decision: to side with Ariel, to follow his heart. The specifics didn't matter.

"He's not the traitor," she added, almost to herself. "He's with us."

SEVEN

187 Puget Drive,
Babylon, Washington
Night of December 21

George Porter had seen a lot of smart people get suckered in his time . . . but this was crazy. How could Ariel and Julia buy Caleb's story? *Anybody* could see through that BS. And these two girls weren't just anybody. Julia had ESP, for God's sake. Ariel was supposed to be the freaking leader of the human race.

He could understand *why* they wanted to believe in Caleb. Obviously. George wanted to believe in him, too. It was no fun worrying that this goofy-looking guy making faces at their baby was really plotting to kill them.

But damn. The whole thing was so clear. The Demon had asked Caleb to steal Ariel's necklace, then sent him on his way with a truckload of toys for the baby? *Please.* Did they all forget that the baby was supposed to be the Demon's worst enemy? It didn't make sense. Caleb was definitely lying about something. Maybe all of it.

And George wouldn't let either Julia or their baby out of his sight until he figured it out.

He had to be sneaky, though. He had to keep his

mouth shut. And for the first time ever, he had to hide his feelings from Julia, which made him even *more* angry. He was even pissed at Ariel. She should have told them that she thought Caleb was the traitor. Earlier. Much earlier. Then George would have been free to be suspicious. Then he could have done something. He could have followed Caleb to the mall or gone through his stuff . . . anything. But now that Caleb was conveniently off the hook, George ended up looking like a jerk for doubting him.

Who knows? Maybe Ariel thinks I'm the traitor now.

Okay, probably not. He was getting paranoid. But he couldn't help it. It was the stress—of trying to take care of this newborn baby, of not sleeping at night, of forcing himself to be polite to Caleb and knowing that he probably wouldn't learn the truth until it was too late.

He couldn't take it much longer. The crying, the fear, the *diapers* . . . He and Julia still hadn't even decided on a name for their daughter.

They hadn't even *thought* about it.

But what stressed him more than anything was the certainty—the inexplicable feeling that had haunted him all year—that their lives as they knew them would be over very soon.

For the first time ever, I know my beautiful baby for who she is. I am so proud. She is the daughter of the one I love, the Sacred Child, the heir of the Chosen One. I stand on the cliff overlooking the ocean. I hold her tightly. I'm not worried she will fall.

*She cries, but her tears don't bring me any pain. They
are tears of joy. The drops flow from those beautiful
eyes. . . .*

And then I hear the Demon laughing.

"I'll see you soon," she says.

I shake my head. "No, you won't. You're scared."

Her laughter dies.

*"You're scared of my baby," I say with a smile.
"That's why you never show your face. You're scared
to get near my daughter."*

*There are footsteps in the gravel behind me. I
turn, but nobody is there.*

"See?" I taunt the Demon. "See?"

*"I don't need to get near your baby to destroy
you," the Demon says. Her voice is like thunder,
crashing down on me from above. "You know it—"*

Something slammed into George's body.

"Ow!" he yelped. He rolled over in the darkness,
blinking, and bumped into the couch. Hadn't he been
sleeping on a couch? His knees and skull were throb-
bing. *Hold up. . . .* He must have fallen onto the
floor.

"George?" Julia whispered hoarsely. "George—are
you all right?"

"Yeah," he muttered, sitting up straight. The floor
was very hard. He blinked a few times and rubbed his
head. *Crap.* He was really out of it.

"I think you were having a bad dream," Julia
murmured.

His eyes narrowed. *A bad dream?* No . . . it was a
vision. A clear vision. He stumbled to his feet, nearly

85

toppling into the crib Caleb had brought home for the baby. *Whoops.* Bad move. He couldn't see a thing. Julia was around here somewhere. All three of them had been sleeping in the living room. . . .

"What was it?" Julia asked.

There she is. A shadow sat up on the sofa opposite the coffee table, behind the crib. He stuck his hands out in front of him like a blind man and dove into the cushions beside her.

"George? Are you sure you're all right?"

He nodded, struggling to sit up straight. "I think I've figured something out," he whispered.

"Tell me." Her delicate fingers felt for his hand, clasping it in her own.

"I think . . . I think our baby can hurt the Demon." He chewed his lip, racking his brain for a way to explain it. "I think she can kill the Demon, actually. Like . . . like, you know how kryptonite is the only thing that can kill Superman? I know that sounds really stupid—but I bet that's one of the reasons our baby is so special."

Julia laughed softly. She sidled closer to him. "That doesn't sound stupid," she whispered.

He sighed and shook his head. "I don't know. Maybe I'm just going crazy. But I feel like my visions really make sense now."

"If you feel that way, then it's probably true," Julia reassured him. "Our feelings are the only things we have, you know?"

"Yeah. Yeah . . . you're right." He nodded, suddenly feeling much more at ease. How did she always manage to pull that off? How could she always manage to calm him, to make him feel as if he were the only guy on earth—and she was the only girl? He was so damn lucky. . . .

"I love you, George," she whispered.

I love you, too. He hugged her against him. He could feel her heart beating against his own chest. *I always will.*

After a few seconds she pulled herself from his embrace. "You know what? We should look for the Demon. What if we just took the baby to the cliff and waited—"

"No," George interrupted. He shook his head. "We can't do that. The baby's only part of the picture. It's like Ariel said: We have to figure out how *she* fits into all of this. And what about your visions? We still don't know about the sword, or the necklace, or the Demon's weapon—or *anything*, really."

Julia was silent for a moment. "But I feel the pull, George." Her voice quavered slightly. "It's worse than ever. I *want* to go to the cliff."

"I know," he soothed. "But we can't go yet. I mean, we *know* that something's supposed to go down on New Year's Eve, right? That's when Caleb said that the Demon wanted the necklace." He swallowed. "I think we should listen to him."

"You still don't trust him, do you?"

In spite of his uneasiness, George had to grin. He should have known Julia could see right through him. He could see right through *her.*

"Do *you?*" he asked.

She took a deep breath. "I don't know," she admitted. "Until now, I figured . . ."

"You figured that Ariel knows best," he finished. He glanced toward the crib—an uncertain black box in the darkness. His *child* was asleep in there. He sighed. "Maybe she does. But I still think we should keep an eye on Caleb."

Julia nodded. "We have to tell Ariel about . . . you know. About the baby, I mean."

"As soon as the sun comes up," George whispered.

She leaned against him again. Funny. He actually felt pretty good. He was wide awake. They were on to something . . . something crucial. The pieces were slowly coming together. For the first time in a very long while, he felt as if he and Julia and Ariel had a real chance at surviving this thing. The Demon *wasn't* all-powerful. Lilith had her own problems and weaknesses—just like the rest of them.

It also helped to know that the girl he loved wasn't a sucker.

Not that he ever really thought she was.

No, the only sucker would be Caleb . . . if Caleb ever tried to double-cross them.

187 Puget Drive,
Babylon, Washington
Early morning, December 22

*And the Chosen One is
blessed with a miracle.*

*Forsaken by the traitor, she
breaks free.*

*But the Demon counterattacks
with magic.*

Ariel rubbed her bleary eyes and groaned. She just
didn't *get* it. Aside from the prophecies in December,
which made absolutely no sense, she could pretty
much figure everything else out . . . except for this
last line about August.

Everything fit up to that point—in *some* way. She
was pretty sure the "miracle" meant surviving
Jezebel's attack. Not that Ariel would call it a miracle. Nightmare was more like it. And she understood
how Caleb had "forsaken" her. Oh, yeah. *Perfectly.*
She wasn't about to forget that. He'd bolted from her
house—not once, but twice . . . and stayed away until
all those kids came to hunt Ariel down. On her eigh-
teenth birthday, no less. Sweet, wasn't it? He had a

good reason, of course. Still, that didn't make the memory any easier to swallow.

But how did Leslie "counterattack with magic"?

For some reason, Ariel had a nasty hunch that the only way to find out would be to ask Leslie herself.

She'd get the chance soon enough. At the big showdown. December 31, 1999. The big New Year's Eve bash. The eve of the millennium. Yahoo!

Wait a second.

Hadn't she sworn to be *out* of Babylon for New Year's Eve this year?

Of course she had. She remembered it well because last year's party sucked—and that was *before* she knew that almost everybody in the world had melted. Oh, well. If she ended up getting slaughtered by the Demon, it couldn't get much worse than listening to Jezebel rant and rave about some car chase or whatever the hell she'd been talking about. . . .

You're getting a little punchy, aren't you?

Yup. Time to crash. It was way too late. She glanced at the Mickey Mouse clock on her bureau, ticking away in the dim candlelight. *Man.* It was almost three-thirty. Her eyes were so achy and fuzzy. . . . If she kept reading at night like this, she'd probably go blind. Every other part of her body seemed to be failing. Her back hurt; her bones creaked; it was all she could do to push herself out of her desk chair and topple into bed.

Ahhh. This stinky mattress had never felt so good. Her eyes fluttered shut. She should have quit a long time ago. Caleb had gotten bored and left—crashing down in Trevor's room again. Too bad. She could use a little snuggling. . . .

My spirit will soon depart my body.

But it will not depart this earth.

The walls of this unholy temple are stained with the blood of a thousand victims. The granite is the color of a rusty blade. The altar of shining onyx has been profaned—laden with idols of Angra Mainyu, in the name of all that is blasphemous and wicked. The graven images stare down upon me. Their grotesque faces mock me. The flames of the sacrificial fire lick at my back, and within moments they will reduce me to ashes.

Yet I will not show fear.

I am at peace even in the face of death. For I am the Saoshyant—the savior, the incarnation of light itself, the human avatar of Ahura Mazda, the Wise Lord. Five hundred years will pass before I reveal the truths to the Prophets and Scribes . . . and three thousand will pass before I walk the earth again.

My spirit will live.

And tragically so will that of Angra Mainyu—of Lilith, as she is known to the nomadic tribes of the Red Sea; of Hecate, as she is known to the shepherds of the Mediterranean.

"Tonight is a glorious night!" the black-robed acolytes sing. "Tonight we commit the Saoshyant's body to fire!"

My body is shackled with heavy chains. Lilith's servants march before me with their flaming torches. But my suffering will end soon. I do not struggle. I accept my fate.

"Tonight truly is a glorious night," a voice whispers in my ear.

The sound is as sweet as the purest note of a flute—as familiar as my own reflection in a still pond. I know it is she. But I will not rest my eyes upon her face.

"Don't you know why it is so special, Saoshyant?" Lilith asks.

I will not meet her gaze!

"Tonight is the longest night of the year. The winter solstice. A truly auspicious occasion. Tonight you begin a long sleep. And so must I. And even when you awaken, you will not remember . . . not until the anniversary of this event."

My breath comes fast. I cannot understand her words. The fire at my back grows hotter, burning my flesh. I turn my head so as not to see the terrible beauty of Angra Mainyu . . . and I find myself drawn to a metal symbol fastened to the base of the altar—a symbol that makes my flesh crawl with revulsion, one of such evil that it can annihilate worlds. . . .

It is the sign of which the ancient magic spoke: two parallel lines, intersecting with two other parallel lines at a slant. Simple. Plain. Meaningless to those who do not understand. But it is Lilith's key to the Future Time—the device that will activate her secret weapon.

I can't let that happen.

One of the servants is staring at me, her face half concealed by torchlight. I can sense the conflict within her, the compassion she feels for me. She is not evil. Only weak. She joined this foul sisterhood out of terror. Many do.

"Destroy the altar!" I hiss. "Smash it and take the key! Hide it for me until the time—"

"Silence!" Lilith bellows. "Tonight you make no demands! Tonight you—"

Ariel bolted upright in bed.

She could hardly breathe. The sheets were damp; her skin and clothing were soaked with sweat. Sunlight poured through the open blinds. It was so damn bright. And that *sound* . . . it was the most horrible, high-pitched screaming she had ever heard. What the hell was going on?

Her heart bounced unevenly. That nightmare—

The baby! Her mind suddenly snapped into focus. Of course. The baby was crying. *Howling.* Like never before. In a flash Ariel threw the covers aside and bounded into the hall.

"Julia?" she called, hurtling down the stairs. "Julia—"

"Sorry," Julia yelled from the living room. Her voice was scratchy, but surprisingly calm. "I didn't mean to wake you up. . . ."

Ariel lurched to a halt at the bottom of the steps, gasping and wide-eyed. She half expected to see some horrible accident. But she didn't. The scene was exactly the same as it was *every* morning. George and Caleb were sprawled across the sofas—while Julia strolled back and forth across the room, jiggling the baby in her arms.

"Shhh," Julia cooed into the baby's ear, raising her voice to be heard over the piercing wail. "You're all right. You're all right."

"Is, uh—is she okay?" Ariel stuttered, frowning.

Julia flashed her a tired smile. "Just a little crankier than usual. That's all. I'm really sorry she woke you up."

Ariel shook her head. "No, no, it's fine. I was just worried. . . ." She gaped at the baby, slack jawed. A little cranky? The kid's tiny face was almost *purple*—shriveled like a raisin and slick with tears. What happened if she got *really* cranky?

"Hey, Ariel, are you okay?" Caleb asked.

"Uh, yeah," she mumbled absently. She brushed her hair out of her eyes. She couldn't stop staring at Julia's daughter. The poor thing was in *agony*. And the dream still clung to her like a bad hangover. Especially the vision of that symbol. What *was* it? The metal piece in the altar was exactly the same as the pendant on her necklace—the Demon's key to the Future Time.

"I'm just a little bugged out. I had a crazy dream. . . ."

"Really?" George sat up straight. He looked nervous. "Me too."

She swallowed. "What was it?"

"It was really a vision," he said. "I learned something. At least I think I did. Leslie's scared of my baby. There's something about the baby that can kill her. And whatever it is, it's the only thing that *can* kill her."

Ariel's eyes narrowed. The only thing? But what about the prophecy?

"Only the tears of humanity can defeat her, brushed upon the Chosen One's sword, which is the Demon's key to the Future Time."

The baby's cries grew softer.

Holy—

And at that moment the answer fell into place—
click!—like a bullet's sliding into the chamber of a
gun.

She knew what the "tears of humanity" were.

She was looking at them. Right at this moment.
They were the tears of the Sacred Child, of Julia and
George's daughter. George had just said it: Something
about the baby could kill Leslie. That something must
be the baby's tears . . . which meant that if Ariel
brushed the necklace's pendant with them, then the
necklace *would* become a sword—a deadly weapon
capable of destroying the Demon.

It fit. All of it. Incredible. The words of the
prophecy actually made *sense*.

"Ariel?" Caleb asked. "Ariel, what is it?"

She smiled—reveling in the same euphoria, the
same *epiphany* that had struck her when she cracked
the code.

Everybody in the room remained frozen . . .
waiting.

"I have a plan," she announced, even before it
was fully formed in her mind. "I know how we're
going to get Lilith."

PART III:

December 31

CHAPTER NINE

187 Puget Drive,
Babylon, Washington
Morning

The days leading up to this moment felt like *weeks* to Caleb.

All he'd done was sit. And stare. And listen to that baby cry.

Last night was the worst, though. The hours plodded through sunrise and beyond, each weighing on Caleb's mind like a year of hard labor . . . but now that he was huddled around the baby's crib with Ariel, George, and Julia—now that he was actually going *through* with Ariel's plan—he made a painful discovery.

He wasn't ready for it.

Not even close. In a way, the endless wait hadn't been long *enough*. This must be how death row prisoners had felt when the hour of execution arrived. Exhausted, but wired. Terrified, but clinging to that glimmer of hope. Praying for a miracle.

He couldn't keep still. He stared down at the sleeping baby—rubbing his palms on his jeans, grinding his teeth. It was cold in here. Really cold . . .

"Are you sure this is gonna work?" George muttered.

Ariel shrugged. "I'm hoping. Like the scroll says, nothing's set in stone."

Caleb swallowed. *Great.* Just what he needed to hear. He turned from the crib and wrapped his arms around himself, glancing out the window. It was another beautiful, sunny day. It hadn't rained all month. Now, *that* was weird. Something was definitely wrong. They were in the state of Washington. The weather should have been crappy. It was an omen. A bad omen. None of them had any idea what they were getting themselves into—

"Hey, Caleb?" Ariel whispered.

He jerked around and blinked at her. "Huh?"

She smiled reassuringly. "I feel good about this, okay?"

"Sure." He attempted a grin, but his lips just ended up twitching. He lowered his eyes to the pendant hanging around her neck. It looked clunky and out of place there . . . but maybe that was because she hadn't worn it in a long time. Or maybe it was because he still couldn't believe that their collective fate rested on *that:* a misshapen metal ticktacktoe board that would sell for fifty cents at a yard sale.

But what if Leslie was telling me the truth?

He shook his head. No. It was the wimp inside him—the wimp who popped out of nowhere, who kept rearing his ugly head. Caleb just had to beat him down. The sniveling little alter ego hadn't even *existed* before. Caleb Walker had always been able to fight fear. Always. He'd faced a thousand sketchy situations over the past year; he'd looked pain and torture and starvation in the eye and never blinked once—

"Caleb?" George muttered. "You all right, man?"

"Yeah, yeah." He nodded unconvincingly. "Fine."

Finally his gaze came to rest on Julia and George's daughter. His jaw tightened. *She* was lucky. All bundled up in little blankets, nestled among a bunch of stuffed animals . . . she had no clue that she might die today. Very soon, in fact. Within hours. Minutes, even.

Unless Leslie was telling me the truth—

The question wouldn't go away. There was no fighting it. It buzzed around his head like an annoying bee. The buzz grew louder and louder—nagging at him, *taunting* him. Because no matter how hard he tried, he couldn't find fault with anything Leslie had said that afternoon. All of it was true. Especially the stuff about Ariel. She wasn't a "pure-as-snow savior." Hardly. She didn't have any amazing powers, either. She was just a *person.*

So maybe it wasn't up to Ariel to save them all.

Maybe it was up to Leslie. *She* was the one who'd destroyed the old world. *She* was the one who'd sent the plague, who could appear and disappear, who could light fires with a snap. . . .

"I guess we should get going, huh?" Julia asked.

Caleb glanced up.

Ariel was staring at him.

Why is she looking at me like that? Oh, crap. I bet she knows that I've been thinking about Leslie. I bet she knows that I've been wondering—

"I guess we should," Ariel mumbled, turning to Julia. "You want to wake the baby up?"

Julia nodded. She took a deep breath, then

reached into the crib and shook her daughter by the leg: once, twice—then a third time, pretty roughly.

"Wake up, sweetie!" Julia called. "Wake up!"

The baby's face wrinkled. Her lips parted . . . and out of that toothless red hole came the all too familiar screech that made Caleb cringe—the cries that had ruined his sleep and chipped away at his sanity every single night this month. . . .

But now he hardly noticed.

Ariel doesn't trust me.

He was certain of it. It was in her eyes. But why *should* she trust him? Leslie was right: He'd betrayed Ariel. He'd *cheated* on her. More than once. And he still hadn't confessed. She still had no idea that he'd fooled around with Jezebel behind her back. Or that he'd fooled around with Leslie other than that first day at the hotel in Seattle. He'd made out with the *Demon*. Several times. And *liked* it. And lied about it. He hadn't known who or what she was at the time . . . but still. There was no excuse. As far as Ariel was concerned, Caleb had been faithful to her from the moment they'd first kissed—all the way back in June.

It was sick. *Sick.*

Always, without fail, the swirling toilet bowl of memories and guilt brought him back to the same question: Why *him?*

Why was *he* caught between the Chosen One and the Demon?

He was nothing more than a random kid—another face in the crowd, a druggie and a fool.

But then, Leslie had been right about another thing, too: Nobody was better than anyone else. Like

George, for instance. The guy was a punk. He didn't strike Caleb as being worthy of fathering some sacred child. But obviously he was. George accepted his role. He *dealt* with it. And what about Ariel? She sure as hell wasn't worthy of being the Chosen One. She was a drunk, a bitch; she'd accidentally murdered her own *mom*. But she was dealing, too. She shoved the bad stuff aside and let the good part shine through.

I've got to do the same thing.

He clenched his fists at his side. Of course he did. He had to end the deception. Leslie might have had a couple of profound things to say about human nature, but she was still responsible for killing every single adult and child on the planet. That was about six billion more people than Ariel could take credit for killing. Six *billion*. What was he thinking, anyway? That number included his parents, most of his friends—almost everybody who had ever mattered to him. No, the difference between Leslie and Ariel was that Leslie was *all* bad. If he was going to die, then he would go out knowing that he'd told Ariel the truth. *All* of it . . .

"You think that's enough tears?" Ariel asked.

Caleb flinched. *Whoa.*

He'd been majorly spacing out. Ariel had already taken off her necklace and was leaning over the crib, gently wiping the baby's face with the pendant. The baby was wailing. Beads of moisture glistened on the dull silver metal.

This was it. They were ready.

"Jesus," George suddenly hissed.

"What?" Ariel asked.

George's eyes grew wide. He stared at Ariel, then at his baby, shaking his head. "I . . ." He turned to Julia. "You *feel* that?"

Uh-oh. Caleb chewed a thumbnail. That didn't sound so good—

"Yeah," Julia whispered tentatively. She was shaking her head, too. She took a few steps back from the crib, nearly tumbling onto one of the sofas. "It's like . . . it's like . . ."

"What?" Ariel demanded. "What's going on?"

Caleb held his breath. He could hear the fear in Ariel's voice. *Oh, jeez—*

"It's like a *release,*" George and Julia answered at the exact same time.

They turned to each other. Smiles broke on their faces.

"I did what I was supposed to do," George whispered, gazing at Julia. His voice rose. "I kept the Demon from getting to my baby. . . ."

"I know, I know!" Julia cried. She stumbled across the room and swept George up in her arms. "My vision's gone, too! I stabbed the Demon! I *did* it! The only—"

"What?" Caleb barked. "What are you talking about?"

"We fulfilled our visions," Julia gasped, closing her eyes and squeezing George as tightly as she possibly could. "We did the right thing. It's like . . . our visions are symbols of things that are supposed to happen in the prophecy. Ariel figured it out. The visions are all part of a bigger picture. We just put the picture together."

"I still don't . . ." Caleb's brow grew furrowed. "What *picture?*"

"The prophecy," George whispered, nodding. He jerked a finger at the wet pendant in Ariel's hands. "That *is* the sword that'll kill the Demon. We're doing the right thing."

"Exactly," Julia said.

Caleb frowned. Didn't they already know that? But the panic began to subside. Maybe there *was* hope. . . .

Ariel's eyes wandered over to George and Julia. "You know what? I think you guys should just wait here with the baby. Caleb and I can handle this on our own—"

"No," they interrupted simultaneously.

Thank God. Caleb's throat clenched. Better to be in a crowd. A *lot* better. Crowds were strong. Couples were weak. He knew *that* from experience.

"We're coming," George declared, stepping apart from Julia. "We still feel the pull. We *have* to go to that cliff with you. All *three* of us. The whole family. That's part of it, too."

"Okay, okay." Ariel bit her lip. She glanced around the room, distracted. "Look, uh, you guys get the baby together, all right? I just . . . um, I want to go outside and clear my head for a sec." She shot Caleb a brief stare, then strode toward the door.

"Me too," Caleb said, reading her cue.

Perfect. She wanted to get him alone. This was the opportunity he'd been praying for: the chance to finally come clean. Everything was going to work out. He was suddenly sure of it. George and Julia had fulfilled their visions. It was as if a thunderstorm had suddenly burst right over his head—drenching him, washing away the fear and self-loathing, *purifying* him. . . .

He followed Ariel out into the sunshine and closed the door. Ariel paused at the end of the walk—right in front of Leslie's black van.

She glanced back at the house, then leaned close to his ear. "Hey, Caleb, are you cool with this?" she whispered. "We don't have to follow my plan."

He hesitated. "What do you mean?"

"I mean, we could just pretend that you never told me anything, that you really *did* steal the necklace. Then you could just hand it over to Leslie. . . ." She frowned and shook her head.

"What?" Caleb pressed. That sounded like a good idea to *him*—so far at least. It was a lot less complicated than what Ariel had in mind. "What's wrong?"

Ariel sighed. "Leslie would see through that. I'm sure she was expecting you to tell me what happened at the mall. Like you said before, she's smart." She stepped back and began nodding to herself. "Yeah, forget it. We have to do it my way. We have to get her to convince *me* to hand it over. *I* have to be the one to give her the necklace."

Caleb ran a hand through his stringy hair. Those feelings of well-being began to fade. He was starting to remember why he'd been so terrified earlier. *"I'm sure she was expecting you to tell me what happened at the mall."* Was he *that* predictable?

"I don't know, Ariel," he muttered. "Can't Leslie read people's minds and stuff? I mean, I didn't want to say this before . . . but won't she know you're lying?"

Ariel managed a grin. "Come on, Caleb. I'm a

pretty good BS artist, aren't I? And I'm *really* good at lying to myself. All I have to do is convince myself that Leslie is telling the truth. Then I'll just hand over the necklace. It's that simple."

He swallowed. That was exactly what Leslie had said about Ariel—that she was good at lying to herself. "It's crazy," he said out loud. "Really crazy . . ."

She shrugged. "We'll see, right?"

And what if Leslie really is telling the truth? he found himself wondering yet again.

He turned away, staring shamefaced at his reflection in the gleaming metal of the van.

Why *had* Leslie given him this van, anyway? So he could bring toys to her mortal enemy? It was completely bizarre. Unless . . . Maybe she was trying to show him that the baby didn't have to be her enemy.

Maybe Leslie *could* control the prophecies. Maybe he was wrong about her being all bad. She'd done nice things for him in the past, right? She'd kissed him. She'd also saved his relationship with Ariel. A bunch of times. Once she'd chased him for twenty miles just to get him to come back home and patch things up with the girl he really loved. . . .

"Is there something you want to tell me, Caleb?" Ariel asked quietly.

He closed his eyes. *Do it! Tell her that you betrayed her!* He drew in a breath . . . but the words just wouldn't come. The truth would crush Ariel. It would destroy the bond between them—at the moment they needed it most. No. He couldn't go through with it.

"Nah," he whispered. He opened his eyes and forced a brave smile. "Let's go."

CHAPTER TEN

The Final Battleground
Noon

The walk from Ariel's house to the cliff wasn't long: ten minutes, fifteen at most. It was a trip Ariel had made a zillion times when she was growing up. As a little kid, she used to go there to fly kites and toss rocks into the ocean. Later she went there to make out with Brian Landau. Then to sneak a couple of beers late at night. Hanging out on the cliff was just a part of growing up in the neighborhood. A lot of other kids had done stuff there, too. It was a great place to catch the sunset. But it wasn't really *special*—at least no more so than any other scenic spot in town.

That's what's so crazy.

The place. The *familiarity*. And the total lack of drama surrounding this moment—at least as far as her environment was concerned.

It was all so . . . mellow. So plain.

Here she was, trudging down the same old two-lane highway with a bunch of kids . . . just as she might have done last New Year's Eve or the one before that. Aside from the baby, nothing was different. Okay, the weather was better. She didn't need a

109

heavy coat. But she could chalk that up to the greenhouse effect, right? It didn't exactly compare to perpetual darkness or swarms of locusts or raining blood. Nope. After a year of catastrophes that strained her imagination, the world looked frighteningly normal, as if nothing had ever happened: The pines were green; the ocean was bluish gray; the tacky chimneys on those mass-produced houses were still ugly . . . et cetera, et cetera.

And we're about to see a Demon who wants to enslave what's left of the human race.

She knew the words were true. But they didn't have any impact. They were just *words*—silly and melodramatic, like a line from a bad script. Anyway, there was no point in trying to fully grasp their *meaning*, their . . . what was the word? Import. Yeah. It couldn't be done. It would be like trying to count to infinity or picture the size of the universe. It was way beyond the scope of Ariel's flawed, pea-sized, and all too human mind.

But Lilith probably understood the circumstances perfectly.

Sure, she did. She didn't have the same limitations as Ariel. Or anyone else, for that matter. She had only one weakness. . . .

This plan is never gonna work, is it?

A shiver shot up Ariel's spine. She glanced at Julia, George, and Caleb. They were all plodding at the same even pace, heads down and faces ashen, as if they were on their way to a funeral. Appropriate, wasn't it? Only the baby looked happy: perched in Julia's grasp and smiling at Ariel with those eyes, those extraordinary eyes, one green and one brown—

"Jesus," George whispered. He paused, eyes wide. "Check it out."

Ariel turned. *Oh, God.*

They'd arrived. And they weren't alone.

Standing in a semicircle on the gravel at the side of the road were what looked like statues of monks. *Female* monks.

There must have been fifty, maybe more—still and silent in long, black, hooded cloaks. . . . Ariel's terrified gaze swept the crowd. They were all gorgeous. Perfect looking. It was insane. But the most frightening thing of all was they were totally expressionless. Their eyes were blank. They didn't even seem to be *breathing*. . . .

"The girls in black robes," Ariel murmured out loud.

Of course. Her stomach squeezed. After hearing all those twisted stories about them, they looked exactly the way she'd imagined. *Exactly.* Like some deranged cult of models—

"What's that—what's that hole in the ground?" Caleb stammered.

Ariel's jaw hung slack. She hadn't even noticed, but the girls were all standing around an enormous pit—maybe ten feet wide.

She stood on her tiptoes to get a better look.

Her heart rate accelerated. Someone was in there. It was too dark to see anything, but there were scuffling noises, the sound of something scraping on rock . . . but she knew who it was even before the figure climbed out of the shadows.

"Whew," Leslie gasped. "They buried this thing deep." She wiped her forehead. In one hand she clutched a shiny black box—about the size and shape of Ariel's old algebra book.

Leslie is not her name, Ariel furiously reminded herself. *That name doesn't exist. It's a trick to hide the truth, just like everything else.*

She couldn't help thinking of her as Leslie, though. Leslie was . . . well, *Leslie*. The carefree smile, that ridiculous miniskirt, those long black curls—they didn't belong to a *demon;* they belonged to a girl, a girl whom Ariel knew . . . her friend.

No. Not my friend. Never—

"Hey!" Leslie cried, waving at Ariel with her free hand. "I knew it. I *knew* you'd be wearing the necklace." She smirked at Caleb. "Never could keep a secret, could you? That's okay. It's better this way. Much better."

Ariel held her breath.

Nobody made a sound.

"The gang's all here, huh?" Leslie went on. She glanced at George and Julia. "You guys couldn't resist the pull. I understand perfectly. The energy that started the clock on this thing was the same that sparked your psychic powers. So you're drawn to it. It's like . . . what's a good analogy?" Her face brightened. "I know. You guys are like flies who can't help but smack right into one of those buzzing electric lights. It's *physics*. It's natural. Living things are drawn to energy sources—"

"Shut up," George barked.

Don't let yourself get worked up, Ariel pleaded.

She's just jabbering. She's screwing with your mind. She's trying to confuse us. . . .

Leslie smirked. "Well, ex-*cuuuse* me. I was just trying to *explain* it. I mean, didn't you ever wonder why you stopped having visions whenever the sun was blocked? It's just—"

"What's in your hand?" Ariel demanded.

Leslie's smile widened. She turned to Ariel and raised her eyebrows. "Why are you being so rude? I haven't seen you in almost two *months.*"

"Answer the question," Ariel spat.

"Oh, come on, Ariel," Leslie quietly chided. "You're a smart girl. Take a guess."

Ariel didn't answer. Her body seemed to wilt.

It's the weapon. That's what it is. That's what's gonna kill us all. That little thing. It's perfect. Almost disappointing. Just like everything else about this day . . .

"I know what you're thinking," Leslie said. She glanced down at the box. "You're thinking that this box looks so *small.* It isn't right somehow. I mean, today is the last day of the millennium. It's supposed to be the end of the world. A big deal. Where's the fire and brimstone? Where's the stuff in the prophecies—the boiling seas and black skies and trembling earth? It just seems weird that it comes down to *this,* right? This little item. After all the huge things that happened to us already: the floods and the rain and the plagues—"

"*You* did that," Ariel growled. "It didn't happen to *you.*" Her lips were trembling. She found she could hardly breathe. This wasn't good. She had to *relax,* to stop listening—at least if her plan had any chance at all of working. . . .

"Wrong, Ariel." Leslie shook her head. "I didn't do any of it. All of those things were way out of my control." A smile crossed her face. "You *know* that. The magic responsible for those disasters is much older than either you or me. It was punishment."

"Punishment?" George shouted. "For *what?*"

Ariel hung her head. Why couldn't they control themselves?

"For the way people screwed up," Leslie replied—but her tone was sympathetic. "You guys had an entire planet to yourselves. You could have done anything with it. You could have made it perfect, and you dropped the ball. You polluted it. You took what it had to offer and used it to kill each other. And the sad thing—the *unfair* thing, really—is that most of you are good people. You're not guilty. But still you had to pay the price." She paused. Her face grew somber. "You're not alone, George. I was punished, too."

"Oh, come off it," Ariel snapped. She didn't care anymore about being played; she couldn't keep a lid on her emotions. "Are you saying we should feel sorry for you? You *used* all those plagues and the rest of that crap for your own good. So don't try to deny it."

Leslie shook her head. "I'm not. But those were just *tools*, Ariel. I was just trimming the fat. Getting rid of the complications. Like the Visionaries. I mean, here are all these kids, having all sorts of crazy flashes . . . and none of them really understand anything." She smiled at George and Julia. "No offense. But it's always been up to Ariel and me. Just the two of us. You know what this really is? This whole year-long mess? It's a misunderstanding between two friends. The problem was that the rest of the world got in the way."

Ariel sneered. *"Please.* The rest of the world got in the way a long time before we became friends. What about the melting plague? Was that a way to 'trim the fat'?"

"Well, *yeah,"* Leslie muttered. "I mean, all those people would have ended up dying, anyway—in all that stuff we've been talking about. I thought I'd take a shortcut and try to bring us together more quickly." She sighed. "Look, Ariel. Let's just get to the point, all right? We don't have much time. I know about the dream you had. So I know that *you* know who you really are. You're the reincarnation of the Saoshyant. The savior, the Chosen One . . . whatever. We met a long time ago in a very different world—in a world where we *couldn't* be friends." Her face softened. "But now we can."

Friends.

The word sliced through Ariel. She literally felt as if it split her in half. In a very real way Leslie *had* been a friend—a soul mate, even. Ariel had never felt closer to anyone else. Not even her own mother. She and Leslie shared the same *insight,* the same humor . . . the same way of looking at people and saying: "Jeez, aren't they easy to figure out?"

Or *had* she and Leslie shared all that?

Maybe not. Ariel couldn't even tell anymore. She had no idea what Leslie was feeling. Did Leslie even have feelings? She had played on Ariel's malicious side—bringing out the worst. But Ariel had to admit something: Even in her frenzied state, even with her fierce resolve . . . it was a lot easier to hate Leslie when she wasn't standing right in front of her.

And what *about* her dream of the past, anyway? Hadn't Ariel tried to tell one of Lilith's servants to steal the symbol in the altar? As if acting of their own free will, Ariel's fingers wandered up to the pendant. And she knew right then, in a burst of clarity, that the symbol she saw on that altar was one and the same as the piece of metal hanging around her neck. . . .

Leslie's dark eyes glittered, stabbing straight into Ariel's own—seemingly right through them. "My servant *did* steal the necklace for you," she said. "And she passed it down through the centuries, just the way the Levys passed the scroll down . . . until that Visionary gave the necklace to you in the hotel. Right in front of me. And you had no idea—"

"Speaking of the Levys, I want to ask you something," Ariel interrupted. Her anger suddenly returned—like a gust of wind, fanning the blaze of a forest fire. She welcomed it. It sharpened her focus. Even if Leslie could read her mind, she couldn't *control* it. "How does Sarah fit into all of this?"

Leslie shrugged. "She doesn't, really. Sarah Levy was never supposed to find the scroll or make it out of Jerusalem. She proved to be pretty tough. A survivor. It was a stroke of bad luck for me." She smiled. "In the same way that Jezebel Howe was a stroke of good luck."

Ariel's eyes narrowed.

"I was lucky enough to have a total psycho living right here in Babylon," Leslie explained matter-of-factly. "A real nutcase. But the amazing thing is that a lot of the things she did matched a lot of the prophecies." She laughed. "I pushed her in the right direction, helping her out with some ESP and stuff, but she really did it herself. You know, I feel kind of bad for her. She just cracked. I guess it was all the death and destruction. . . ."

Oh, my God. Ariel's heart lurched. She couldn't believe it. All that time she thought that Jezebel was evil, a bitch . . . just an exaggeration of her normal self. A sickening wave of guilt swept over her. Obviously Jezebel had no idea what she was even doing. And Leslie had taken advantage of that. *I'm so sorry, Jez. I'm so sorry—*

"Ariel, listen to me," Leslie pleaded in the silence. Her tone grew serious again. She stepped out onto the road. "It doesn't have to be like that anymore. Nobody has to suffer. Nobody else has to die of the plague, either. The virus is gone; it only had a life of about ten months or so. We don't even need the antidote. We can start over. Today. *Now.* All of us."

Ariel stared down at the pavement. The necklace gleamed in the noon sunlight. She couldn't respond. With every comment Leslie made, with every new revelation, Ariel's hope dwindled more and more. She didn't even know what she was *thinking.* . . .

"You've looked at the prophecies," Leslie continued. "You know that nothing is absolute. All that stuff about 'enslaving' people—it's all garbage. The Scribes wrote that crap because they thought that the world was divided into two halves: right and wrong. Period. But we've come a long way since then. You and I both know it. So we have to take what's left of the world and make it a better place—a world of freedom, of understanding. We'll be able to do what feels *good* without having to worry about some random system of morals . . . a system made up by hypocrites. *They're* the ones who wanted to enslave you. Not me."

"But—but what about all those people you killed?" Ariel stammered. She couldn't bring herself to meet Leslie's gaze. "Isn't that bad?"

"It was bad that they had to die," Leslie answered gravely. "But like I said, they would have died, anyway. *They* were the people who created the old system. *They* were the ones who ruined the old world. And the Scribes were part of that world. Don't let their words fool you. It's up to us to change things. Think about it. You and me, side by side. The Scribes would never have *conceived* of such a thing." Her voice grew dreamy. "Two chicks. Girl power, babe! No more sexism or prejudice or anything. Just equality. It'll be paradise. We can be one. The same. Everybody. With you and me at the top."

Finally Ariel forced herself to lift her head. "All I have to do is give you the necklace?"

Leslie nodded. She took another few steps forward and extended the black box, holding it out to Ariel as if it were an offering. There was a slim opening on one end—barely visible, a slit of utter darkness.

"It's not a weapon," Leslie murmured, almost lovingly. "It's a *cure*. A gift. The pendant fits inside. It has to be placed there at exactly the right moment. That's what the countdown is all about. It ends today. Soon. And if everything works out, this box will release all the pent-up energy of the solar flare. That energy will give everyone eternal life, Ariel. You and me already have it. I'm talking about the rest of the world. We can all live forever."

Ariel swallowed. She closed her eyes. Eternal life? She never *wanted* that. In her mind she could glimpse the "paradise" of which Leslie spoke . . . and all she saw was emptiness: a bleak landscape where individuality ceased to exist, where the Demon controlled every thought and action. Leslie didn't want Ariel to rule at her side. No. Leslie wanted the survivors to become an extension of herself, like those girls in black robes. The Scribes were right. Leslie's only desire was for Ariel to be her slave . . . for *everyone* to be her slave.

Ariel tore the pendant from her neck. The broken chain fell to the ground.

"Here you go," she whispered: "It's all yours."

And with that, she tossed the pendant into the air—straight at her old friend.

The Blind Moment

The key to the Future Time twirled end over end, glittering in the sunlight like a shooting star—and as Ariel followed the arc of its flight, it seemed to her that the passage of time began to flow in reverse. Her mind raced down the corridors of the past year, back through the pain and solitude and suffering . . . until she saw herself strolling through those hotel doors in Seattle and laying eyes on Leslie for the first time.

The memory had never been clearer.

"And you must be Caleb's little friend."

Those were the very first words Leslie had ever spoken to her. All the while, during that first encounter, Leslie had *known*—that Ariel was the Chosen One, that Ariel was her rival of three thousand years. She'd even introduced herself by her full name: Leslie Arliss Irma Tisch. Her real name was hidden in there as well. So in a way, she'd told Ariel the truth from the moment they met. Lilith had confessed her identity to the Chosen One. But it was her genius to hide it at the same time. She did that with everything—as Ariel did herself, to some degree. Maybe Leslie really *wanted* to be the same as Ariel. . . .

"You made the right choice, Saoshyant!" Leslie cried gleefully.

The moment was over.

Ariel's gaze flashed back to the Demon . . . to Leslie, to Lilith, to her most bitter enemy and best friend. Leslie's arms were outstretched; her black eyes had glazed over in delight. She clutched the weapon in her right hand. With her left, she reached out and deftly plucked the pendant from the air as it flew over her head.

"Yes!" she cried. "Now I—"

Her face soured.

Her eyes widened. "What the—"

"Drop it, Leslie!" Caleb shrieked.

Ariel's head jerked. She'd completely forgotten about him . . . about George and Julia and the baby—even about the girls in black robes. The rest of the world had faded. But now Caleb was scrambling toward the cliff, shaking his head and waving his arms like a lunatic.

Panic took hold of Ariel. *No, no.* He would ruin everything. He would destroy the plan—

The traitor.

Blood turned to ice in her veins.

The prophecies were coming true. The traitor was serving the Demon in the Final Hour—

"Drop it!" he yelled. "Drop it. . . ."

The next moment George was sprinting after him. Ariel only saw a whir of pumping legs. He caught up to Caleb in a matter of seconds. Lowering his shoulder, George slammed directly into the small of Caleb's back—and the two of them went sprawling to the pavement.

"Leslie!" Caleb shrieked helplessly. "Let it go! It's a trick!"

But Leslie was frozen, still clutching the weapon and the key over her head—her pristine features twisted in a scowl, her full red lips parted in surprise. Only . . . something was happening to her body.

The flesh on her arms seemed to be *shimmering* slightly—puckering in little ripples, as if she were made of liquid. She turned a ghastly white. The black box fell from her grasp.

"No!" she roared.

Ariel winced. The sound was deafening, inhuman—almost like the cry of an animal. But there was terror in it. . . .

In an instant the crowd of servants closed in around Leslie, shielding her from sight. A mournful wail rose into the salty ocean air. They stumbled over one another, clawing at one another's robes in a desperate effort to reach her. And as Ariel stared at them, she knew that she had succeeded. There was no saving the Demon now. The tears of the Sacred Child had worked their magic—ironically destroying Lilith in almost the exact same gruesome fashion as the plague had killed all those billions of innocent people.

"You *killed* her!" one of the servants shrieked, whirling. "You ruined everything! Now *we* have to . . ." Her voice was lost in the screaming.

Uh-oh. Ariel bit her lip. Leslie might be lying dead in the middle of that huddle, but somebody could still easily put the key in the weapon. Without thinking, she dashed forward and lunged headfirst into the crowd—shoving the girls aside with her arms, kicking them with her legs.

"Wait!" Julia cried.

The baby started howling.

"Don't go in there!" George shouted.

Ariel ignored them. She viciously forced her way through the mob until she stood panting over what remained of Leslie's body. She cringed. There was very little left. Only a puddle of blood . . . blood that bubbled and burned with flames. So Leslie was really gone. But there was no time to think about that. The black box and pendant lay in the midst of the dancing liquid fire. Steeling her nerves for pain, Ariel thrust her arms into the blaze and snatched out the weapon and the key.

My God!

She didn't feel a thing . . . other than a pleasant warmth, like the heat of the sun.

And then she remembered.

She couldn't be hurt or killed.

All at once the hooded girls stopped jostling one another.

They gaped at Ariel. Their cries fell silent. They began to back away from her, away from Lilith's melted remnants. A few tumbled to the gravel, their faces etched with fear.

Now's my chance, Ariel realized. *They're scared of me. Now I can get rid of this stuff forever.* Her eyes darted toward the vast expanse of the ocean. She jumped over the fire and ran to the edge of the cliff.

"Ariel, no!" Caleb shouted.

With one fluid motion she hurtled the box and the necklace far out over the precipice.

The two artifacts hung in the air for a moment,

then began to fall through open space, gaining speed and momentum—faster and faster . . . until they disappeared in the wild froth of the crashing waves far below.

Ariel sank to her knees.

It's over.

She shivered. Her lungs heaved.

It didn't seem possible that Lilith was truly *dead*—that her weapons were lost, that she would never befriend anyone else or make any more false promises ever again. But it was true.

Lilith's reign was over before it started.

Ariel glanced over her shoulder at the assembled multitude. They stared back at her in horror.

Her eyes hardened.

They deserved to be scared. They deserved to be *punished,* too. But they didn't deserve to die—or even to become slaves. Nobody did. Not even Lilith. But Lilith had brought her own fate upon herself. . . .

Caleb!

He suddenly lurched out from behind them. His body was limp, flaccid; his face was moist with tears. George chased after him.

"Why did you *do* it?" Caleb sobbed as he staggered toward Ariel. "Why did you kill her? She could have been telling the truth—"

"Shut the hell up!" George barked.

Ariel raised a hand and shook her head. "No, no. It's okay."

"You could have done something," Caleb wept, collapsing onto the gravel beside her. "It didn't have to be like that. Weren't you listening to what she

Gradually, with trepidation, the girls edged toward Ariel. Julia stood among them, patting the baby's head. Lilith's servants didn't even seem to notice that the child was there—that they were crowded next to this Sacred Being whose tears had destroyed their master. Maybe they were in a state of shock. Or maybe they had simply resigned themselves to the fact that the battle was over. They were no longer enemies. Like Lilith had said herself: They were all one. The same. *All* of them. Everyone on this cliff. They were all survivors, casualties. . . .

"I just want to say a few things," Ariel stated. Her voice was hoarse. The sea breeze rustled her hair. "I didn't want to kill her—I mean it. I know that sounds weird. She was . . . she was my friend." She tried to swallow, but a large lump clogged her throat. She gazed at the girls gathered around her. Their faces appeared softer somehow—more human. "But Lilith didn't leave me a choice. She wanted to destroy us—and by us, I mean *people*." Her eyes flashed to Julia's baby. "And I couldn't let that happen, right?"

A girl stepped out of the crowd. She pulled back her hood. Long black hair cascaded down to her waist. Her eyes were like ice. "Lilith didn't want to destroy us," she hissed. "She wanted to *save* us. You didn't—"

"Amanda!" George bellowed. He took three quick steps toward her and shoved her back against a couple of others. "I should *kill* you—"

"Stop," Ariel cried. *"Please,* okay? Just let me talk."

He stood still, breathing heavily, his eyes flashing between the two of them.

Ariel's brow grew furrowed. *Wait a second.* George had called that girl by name.

"You *know* each other?" she asked.

George nodded. He glared at the girl. "She tried to kill me and Julia. Back in February. She told me that all Visionaries must die—"

"It's okay, George," Ariel soothed. She struggled to her feet and stood between them. "This is exactly what I wanted to talk about. See, every single one of us was manipulated." She glanced at the girl, then back at George. Their expressions were smoldering, but neither said a word. "We were all pawns in this huge scheme. Somewhere, at some time, Lilith fooled all of us. Every single one."

The girl shook her head. "Not me—"

"Yes, you. You spent the whole year trying to kill all those people because you thought that Lilith would give you some huge reward at the end. But that wasn't part of her plan. She had to use you to get what she wanted. And all she wanted was for us to serve her for the rest of our lives—to *control* us. Totally."

"I would have served her," the girl whispered.

Ariel shrugged. "I know you would have. You wouldn't have had a choice." She sighed. "Lilith knew what buttons to push. She knew all about people. Most of that stuff she said was true. The world *was* screwed up. We did it to ourselves. We *should* start over. And we should recognize what we did wrong so we won't make the same mistakes. Just like Lilith said."

"Like *Lilith?*" George cried. "But—"

"She was right on, George. I mean . . . just look at *me*, right? I'm the Chosen One. And I'm just as much of a mess as anyone else. But if we just start telling the truth about ourselves, then we won't have to put on these stupid acts anymore. It was all of our *lies* that made the world go wrong. Without them we can make a fresh start."

Caleb rubbed his eyes and sniffed, gazing up at her. "You honestly *believe* that?"

"Yeah, I do," Ariel answered firmly. "All of us here can start. 'Cause we're the last generation. We're the last of the hypocrites, the last of the bad." She pointed at Julia's baby. "And *she's* the first of the good. She's a clean slate. What's that saying? *Tabula rasa.* Yeah. She doesn't know what the old world was like—and she never will, at least not firsthand. So it's up to us to make it as perfect as possible for her. We *can't* make it perfect because we're human. But we owe it to her to try as hard as we can."

"And how do we do that?" the girl demanded.

Ariel waved her hand at the tree-lined road behind them. "You head out from here and spread the word to all the rest of the survivors—all the rest of the kids like us." She shot a hard stare at the girl. "That's *your* punishment. You're gonna spend the rest of your lives traveling the world, telling everyone the truth about yourselves and what happened so we never make the same mistakes again." She glanced back at Julia's baby. "You're gonna tell them about how Lilith was destroyed by this little girl. About how the pure tears of a newborn baby wiped out the evil of the past."

The girl didn't answer. She bowed her head.

Don't feel so bad, Ariel thought, turning back out to the ocean. The waves blended into the cloudless sky in a light blue haze at the horizon—a seamless and infinite expanse of space. *I have my own punishment. My punishment is eternity. Now that Lilith's weapon is gone, I'm going to live forever. And I'm going to spend forever making sure that the world is a very different place.*

"Hey, Ariel?" Caleb murmured. "What about the end of the prophecies? Remember what it said about the trembling earth and boiling seas? Is that still gonna happen?"

Ariel took a deep breath of the crisp Pacific air. "I don't know. I guess we'll just have to see." She blinked. A strange, wistful sadness spread through her body. She knew then that it was over between her and Caleb . . . that in a way, it had been over a long, long time ago. There had never really been any trust between them. Like everything else of the past, their relationship represented the old world—a world of hypocrisy that no longer existed, that *couldn't* exist.

It was time to start over.

She turned back to Julia. "You know, you guys never named your baby."

Julia smiled at her. "Yes, we did. We just never told you. Her name is Ariel."

Keys to the Future

February

Reshape Time. In their own distress, help ends soon. A light is a dear aura. 2,20,99.

March

To be heavenly raises us. Deals make it safer for all fools to read lips. Three twenty-seven ninety-nine.

April

Fearing a rotten end, scaring a pig with songs, the evil eye brings the terror to the red box and atlas. Four one ninety-nine.

May

Lift our scale unless we trip, so drink in our volcano. Adultery stirs him. We demand a marker for strikes. Five two ninety-nine.

June

Strong floods wait by a blue bath and poke seeds at the seas. The whale eats eggs and drops teeth. Six twenty-one ninety-nine.

July

Truth never rests in honor, now that man understands a sign to be or to battle a poor coward. Seven seventeen ninety-nine.

August

Each artery in the thin squid unseals a knife. Eat sufficiently. Then hunger is wasted on sport. Eight twenty-six ninety-nine.

September

A shovel can help change news. Cut the pie and save it. Run for the choice to cry. Stone a clock to miss delays. Nine nine ninety-nine.

October

Depraved rats known to feed as one soon bury lethal sins of killers. Steal some tan cheese and sneak away. Ten twenty-two ninety-nine.

November

Tough care mends flaws. Try to kill nondefensive spells. Slips affect sins. Eleven twenty-three ninety-nine.

Meteors ruin an empty forest. An animal noisily seeks relief. Foxes appeal unto wedded demons. Eleven twenty-five ninety-nine.

December

Moreover, every dead eater will bring a violent trap as the Healer, in rhythmic evil, is far. Twelve two ninety-nine.